The Hell with Elaine

The Hell with Elaine

Van Siller

PUBLISHED FOR THE CRIME CLUB BY

DOUBLEDAY & COMPANY, INC.

GARDEN CITY, NEW YORK

1974

All of the characters in this book
are fictitious, and any resemblance
to actual persons, living or dead,
is purely coincidental.

Library of Congress Cataloging in Publication Data

Van Siller, Hilda.
  The hell with Elaine.

  I. Title.
PZ3.V3625He [PS3543.A648] 813'.5'4
ISBN 0-385-08900-7
Library of Congress Catalog Card Number 73–10978

Siller

The Hell with Elaine

Neil Stratton sat stoically regarding the empty glass clutched in his hand. He could have used another scotch, but he knew that if he got up someone would grab his spot on the sofa, so he endured the cocktail prattle of a heavily perfumed woman twice his age, who was pitching her voice high over the other party voices. He already knew that she designed hats, had been married twice and had known their host and hostess, the Oliver Vails, for years.

"How long have you known them?" she asked brightly, apparently desperate to keep some kind of conversation going.

"A couple of years," he said.

He had spent most of the day in Connecticut trudging around wholesale nurseries examining trees and shrubs he might use for the Moncrief project. The mid-September day which he had hoped would be clear and sunny, had started off with fog and gone into a steady drizzle. It had lasted all day and through the long drive back to New York. He was damp and uncomfortable and his feet hurt. He would not have bothered coming, except for the fact that it was Andrew Crawford's birthday and Andrew was Kate Vail's father.

He was also president of Crawford, Gordon, Kingman and Lawrence, Attorneys, who specialized in handling the affairs of wealthy clients and administering their estates. Neil had never been more surprised in his life than when he had found out that his grandmother, Nellie Power, had been one of their clients and he had only found it out the year before, when she died.

Neil had known that Nellie had a lawyer, a man named Harrison, who sometimes called at her rather shabby but scrupulously clean apartment on Riverside Drive, but he had assumed that the thin, solemn man came from some unimportant neighborhood firm which handled the small business affairs of nice old ladies, perhaps calling more often than necessary to collect further fees.

Even when Harrison had retired and Robert Ewing had taken his place about a year before Nellie's death, Neil had not associated him with anyone but Harrison. Neither his grandmother nor Harrison had ever discussed her finances with Neil and Bob did not either. But he, unlike his predecessor, was young and friendly and Neil liked him right off. Both bachelors in their mid-twenties, they found they had a lot in common and became close friends. It had been through Bob that Neil had met the Vails long before he knew that Kate's father had ever heard of his grandmother.

It was only after Nellie's death that he learned Harrison had been a senior member of the Crawford firm and Bob, a very junior one. Both men had known all along that upon Nellie Power's death, Neil would inherit an estate of considerable size, but at her instructions he was not to know until she was gone.

After years of scrimping and reluctantly accepting his grandmother's help in getting through Cornell and finally setting up as a landscape architect, he still could not really believe he was a rich man. He had swapped his one-roomer for a penthouse in the East Sixties not far from Fifth Avenue and got a tremendous kick out of planting his garden-terrace, but it still seemed like some lovely dream that might vanish with the dawn.

So here he was, waiting to pay his respects to Andrew Crawford and bored to death. For some reason he had expected a smallish party, but realized the minute he got there that crafty Andrew had dumped a mess of his social and business obligations on his daughter and son-in-law, a habit he had developed since his wife's death. Neither Kate nor Oliver seemed to mind. They liked people and Oliver was in public relations, where all kinds of contacts might prove useful.

"Doesn't Kate look simply fabulous with that new hairdo?" the hat designer asked.

He looked through the crowd of people standing around, trying to juggle their drinks and canapés and cigarettes while they shouted at each other and laughed inordinately. He saw Kate's head briefly, noticed that her dark hair was now short with wings of white, setting off her perpetually tanned face, her radiant, white smile. A group of people moved aside and he saw that the smile was directed toward a girl with light brown hair, windblown bangs and a slim figure. They were standing by the bar, drinks in hand, and Kate seemed to be introducing the girl to a couple near them.

Neil stared at the girl. He knew he had never laid eyes on her before, but there was something terribly familiar about her. Perhaps it was the way she used her hands, holding her drink in one and making vague little gestures with the other. Or it might have been the way she smiled or held her head a little to one side when she listened.

Elaine, he thought.

"What's the matter, dear?" the woman beside him asked. "You look as though you'd seen a ghost."

"Do you know that girl with Kate?"

"The one in the little black suit. No, but I bet that suit is a . . . Oh, there's Andrew. It's his birthday, you know." She reached down and took a huge black patent purse and a gaily wrapped package from the floor at her feet. "Coals to

Newcastle. A bottle of scotch. Couldn't think of another bloody thing."

Neil saw Andrew too, standing with a cluster of people, smiling, polished, his plumpish body encased in a beautifully cut gray suit, his bronzed head shining under his sparse silver hair. Andrew lived in Greenwich and spent as much time on the golf course as in his office, but he was far from retired. Neil watched the hat designer wend her way through the thinning mob, then a maid finally showed up with a tray of drinks and he seized another scotch. When he looked back toward the bar, he could see neither Kate nor the girl.

He sat there brooding, thinking of Elaine and furious because he was. It was getting late and people were starting to leave in earnest. He thought of pushing his way to Andrew, wishing him a happy birthday and clearing off, but somehow he had to see that girl again. Besides, he had his new drink and was beginning to feel human again. He brooded and sipped and then saw the girl talking to Paul Kendell, a skinny red-haired fashion photographer he had met a few times. The girl's profile was delicate, her expression animated and while there was no physical resemblance she still made him think of Elaine.

He was so intent on watching her that he did not notice the well-built young man who slid into the seat beside him.

"What's so damned fascinating?" the young man asked.

Neil turned to see Bob Ewing plucking an olive from a martini.

"It's that girl over there," he said. "The one talking to Paul Kendell."

Bob adjusted his horn-rimmed glasses and peered across the room. "Never saw her before. What's so earthshaking about her?" he asked, and popped the olive into his mouth.

"I don't know why, but she reminds me of Elaine."

"Elaine?" Bob stopped chewing, frowned and squinted at the girl, then turned back to Neil.

"You're crazy. She's nothing like Elaine. She's shorter and much smaller boned. Pretty, but she hasn't got that classical beauty. I don't see any resemblance at all."

"It's just the mannerisms, I guess, but there is something . . ."

"I'd hoped you had forgotten about Elaine," Bob said, his expression suddenly serious.

Neil flushed and his Irish blue eyes darkened. Bob saw it and swiftly changed the subject.

"How's the Moncrief job coming on?" he asked.

"All right, but these developers never leave enough space for planning and proper landscaping. The drainage might be a problem, too."

A year ago, Neil could never have taken on the Moncrief job, a development of expensive houses in upper Westchester. He had studied engineering in college, but had switched to landscaping and planning when he realized what a hideous mess Americans seemed bent on making of the country. After his windfall, he had taken a partner, Allen Rutland, an older, more experienced man with a good following and sweeping ideas. They had opened offices on East Fifty-seventh and were now Stratton and Rutland, Landscape Architects and Planners.

Bob laughed. "Your trouble is that you want to make the whole world beautiful. You'd plant trees up and down Broadway if they'd let you."

"You're damned right I would."

"Got anything on later?" Bob asked. "I'm meeting Carol for dinner. We'd be glad to have you join us if you'd like to."

Like hell you would, Neil thought. Carol was a pretty blonde Bob had been dating for the past six months or so, a long time for a man who played the field. During the two years they had known each other, Bob had gone around with at least a dozen girls. Elaine had been one of them and it had been here in this room that Neil had first met her. Perhaps that was why . . .

"Well, what about it?" Bob asked.

"Thanks, but I told Mrs. Mallory I'd be home for dinner."

Bob finished off his martini. "Well, I'd better congratulate the boss and get going. Late now." He got up, ran his fingers through his dark hair and frowned down at Neil. "For God's sake, don't sit around moping about Elaine."

Neil nodded, but that was exactly what he did. He thought of the party, another like this, only in the very early spring about a year and a half ago when Bob had turned up with a beautiful girl who had the features of a Greek goddess and a figure to match. Her long black hair had been parted in the middle, her lips full and sensuous, her dress the color of rubies.

Bob had presented her with a wide grin. "Look what I found . . . in the office of all places. Her father is a friend of Andrew Crawford's."

"A very old friend," the girl said. "They were in college together."

"Elaine Parker, Neil Stratton," Bob said briefly.

She tilted her head and smiled, a cool, but sexy little smile which unnerved him. He had been interested in her right away, but had not pursued it, because she was Bob's find. Once or twice he got another girl and they all went out together, but it was several weeks before he saw her alone, and then by accident.

He had just come out of the old building on Lexington where his office had been at the time and had almost run into her. He'd had little cash at the time, but he had invited her to dinner and taken her to Twenty One, a wild extravagance then. Later she had told him there was nothing between her and Bob.

"When my parents were divorced years ago, Mr. Crawford arranged the property settlement. Part of it was a beach house on the Sound not far from Westport. My mother got it with the stipulation that my father keep up the taxes and insurance as long as she or I kept the property. My mother died several years ago, so it's mine now. I've been in California and the place has been closed, but I found out that nothing had been paid, so I went to see Mr. Crawford. He had Bob take care of things and that's how I met him."

"Are you still seeing him?"

She shook her head. "I moved out to the beach house. It's early in the season and gets quite cold, but I like the peace and quiet. I need it for my work."

"Work?"

She smiled, but her dark eyes were grave. "Don't die laughing, but I write poetry."

It turned out that she was twenty-four and a high-priced fashion model, but she had gotten tired of it and tried acting in Hollywood, which hadn't worked out, so she had returned to New York. Now she was modeling two or three days a week to support herself and writing poetry the rest of the time.

"Don't you get lonely or scared living out there alone?" he had asked, thinking of girls he knew who wouldn't walk through Central Park alone at night for the Hope diamond.

"No, I like it. The summer people haven't come yet and I can walk on the beach at night when I get stuck. I love to listen to the rhythm of the waves."

They had gone out on the town after dinner that night and got a little high and then it had been too late for her to get back to Westport, so she spent the night with him in his one-roomer. It had been the most glorious night of Neil's life and he fell in love with her blindly. She was cool and at times a little remote, as though keeping some part of herself a secret from him, but she had been wonderful to make love to. That was how it began.

God, he thought, draining his drink, if he had only known then how it would end. His thoughts broke off abruptly as he saw Kate approaching with the girl in tow. He got up and would have bolted, but Kate's eyes told him he was the target. He had wanted to meet the girl, but thinking of Elaine made him leery of another entanglement. But it was too late.

"Neil, I'd like you to meet Nancy Gilbert. Nancy, this is Neil Stratton." Kate flashed her white smile. "Now, you kiddies have a drink while I rescue my father before he drowns in champagne."

She took off immediately, leaving Neil and the girl standing awkwardly.

"Won't you sit down?" he asked.

She smiled and sat down, crossing her slim legs. The maid turned up again with more drinks. Neil offered Nancy a cigarette and lit one for himself too, stalling. He had seen the veiled curiosity in her blue-green eyes and wondered how much Kate had told her about him.

"I haven't seen you around before," he said, finally. "Do you live in New York?"

"I just got back from Rome a week ago."

"Nice trip?"

"It wasn't exactly a trip. I've been abroad for several years. My mother took me to Europe to find me a husband, but I found one for her." Nancy laughed. "I married her off last month."

"That's a switch," he said.

She took a sip of her drink and regarded him over the rim of the glass, the curious look still lurking in her eyes; then she lowered the glass.

"Kate tells me that you were engaged to Elaine Parker," she said.

He almost jumped out of his skin, but managed to take a long drag on his cigarette and nod. She couldn't know that his heart was suddenly pounding and he had begun to sweat.

"Do you know Elaine?" he asked.

"Yes, but I haven't seen her for ages. A friend of mine asked me to look her up when I got to New York, but I can't find her. I was wondering if . . ."

"The last time I saw her she was living in Westport, Connecticut, but I understand she closed the house and came back to New York over a year ago. I haven't seen her since then."

Nancy took another sip of her drink. "This friend thought Andrew Crawford might know where she was because he handled some business for her father, but he hasn't seen her for a long time either. That's why he invited me here. He thought some of her friends might be here. I haven't met the Vails before. Lovely couple, aren't they?"

"Yes."

She saw him looking at his watch. "Am I keeping you from something, Mr. Stratton?"

"As a matter of fact, my housekeeper is expecting me home for dinner at seven-thirty and it's after seven. I always try to be on time."

"Oh."

He glanced sideways and saw her looking down at her glass. There was something childish about her profile—the short nose and wispy bangs, probably. Then he realized that she seemed hurt by his curt answer to her question. How could anything about her have reminded him of Elaine? And then it occurred to him that if she had been abroad for years and just returned, she probably didn't know many people in the city and had nothing to do for the rest of the evening.

"Would you like to come and have dinner with me?" he asked.

She brightened instantly. "I'd love to."

He phoned Mrs. Mallory while Nancy got her things and then they waited in the cold drizzle while the doorman blew frantically trying to get them a cab, but the arrogant drivers swished by, sending out sprays of muddy water, their passengers invisible behind dark, misted windows. They were on Park at Sixty-first, and had to walk down to Fifty-seventh before they found a cab.

His penthouse, when they finally arrived, had never looked more warm and inviting. Mrs. Mallory, a plump, sturdy woman with suspiciously dark hair and soft eyes, had lit the fire and drawn the curtains against the miserable night outside. There was ice out and various bottles on the bar. Mrs. Mallory welcomed them and took their things, then smiled at Nancy.

"It's so nice to have company on such a nasty night," she said, then hurried out to the kitchen to see about dinner.

"Aren't you lucky to have such a nice housekeeper?" Nancy said. "She looks like an old dear."

"She is."

Neil made the drinks while Nancy stood by the fire, warming her hands. She made a pretty picture with her light brown hair and slim figure in the trim little suit, standing there with the firelight behind her.

"What a lovely room," she said, looking around at the comfortable furniture, vases of fresh flowers and paintings, mostly landscapes. "It seems more like a country house than an apartment."

"That's the idea." He waved toward the drawn curtains. "There's a garden out there, but it's probably drowned tonight."

When he carried their drinks over to the cocktail table in front of a sofa which faced the fire, Nancy joined him and for some reason it seemed natural to have her there. Perhaps it was the fire hissing gently while the drizzle outside had turned to rain and was beating against the french doors, or the scent of a roast drifting in from the kitchen. Whatever it was, he felt happy and relaxed and was glad he had invited her. Then she ruined it.

She looked around the expensive, well-appointed room and then at him. "Elaine must have been crazy not to marry you," she said. "All this and you too."

"I didn't have this apartment then and I never expected to," he snapped.

Nancy's eyes widened. "But Kate said you'd inherited a lot of money from your grandmother. Didn't you know you would get it?"

"No," he said, looking into the fire. "My grandmother was a servant like Mrs. Mallory, a housekeeper. I never dreamed she had any money."

Nancy tilted her head to one side and smiled cozily. "Why, that's fascinating. Tell me about it."

He had been forced to tell the story so many times that he could rattle it off like a record. He did not enjoy doing it, but the story had been widely publicized and people were always curious about it.

"She came over from Ireland before the First World War and got a job as a maid," he said. "Her name was Nellie O'Neil. That's where I got my name. She married a man she met on the boat coming over, but he turned out to be a drunk and went back to Ireland, leaving her with a little girl to support. Nellie put her daughter in a convent and worked her head off cooking and scrubbing and scrimping."

"And the little girl was your mother," Nancy said, like a child listening to a bedtime story.

He nodded. "She grew up and married a soldier in the regular army. He was stationed in Germany when I was born and he died there, so I never saw him. My mother died when I was six, so Nellie was the only mother I ever really knew."

He paused, bored with the whole thing.

"But your grandmother . . . all that money?" Nancy looked puzzled.

"Nellie kept working and became a housekeeper for a family named Winterson. Max Winterson was a very successful investment broker and he took an interest in Nellie's affairs. His wife was an invalid and Nellie ran his house for years and all the time she was investing her money and following his advice. She bought real estate when it was cheap and stocks and bonds and all sorts of things."

Nancy's eyes were even wider. "And you never knew?"

"No, not until she died. She had a small apartment on Riverside Drive and she put me in a boarding school. She sent me to camp in the summer and I spent my holidays with her, but everything was always frugal. She never spent anything on herself and I never thought she had anything beyond a savings account or perhaps some small investments against her old age. All those years I thought she was scrimping and doing without things to help educate me and get me started and I felt awful taking it from her."

"Why on earth didn't she tell you?"

Neil smiled, thinking of his little grandmother's impish blue eyes. "She loved surprises. Andrew Crawford thinks it was to be the great surprise and that she spent years enjoying it before she died, but I think it was watching what money did to Winterson's sons when they were young. She thought it ruined them. They were brought up with everything, but one of them went to jail for fraud and the other committed suicide."

He leaned back and lit a cigarette. "Well, now you know. Before Winterson died, he arranged to have the Crawford firm look after Nellie's investments, and they did. And when she died, I got it all. That's about it. It took me weeks to get over the shock. Sometimes I still can't believe it."

Mrs. Mallory came in and announced dinner then. The roast turned out to be excellent and Mrs. Mallory, having been trained by a friend of Kate Vail's, knew which wines to serve and how to serve them. When they returned to the living room, she brought them coffee and Neil poured some of his best brandy. They sat in front of the fire, enjoying its dancing flames and warmth and then Nancy killed the mellow mood again.

"Then Elaine didn't know you were going to inherit a lot of money?" she asked.

He frowned impatiently. "How could she? I didn't know myself. I met her in late March and we started going together a few weeks later. We were going to get married, but in August we broke up. My grandmother died a month or so after that. Now, for God's sake, let's stop talking about Elaine."

Nancy gave him a searching glance. "Why? Are you still in love with her?"

He finished off his cognac in one gulp and put the glass down with a bang. "I loathe her guts," he said, and then his eyes narrowed. "How much did Kate tell you about Elaine and me?"

"Oh, I've heard all sorts of things," she said vaguely, curling up against a cushion, "but you have to take gossip with a grain of salt. Were you very much in love with her?"

He did not want to go on with it, but he realized that he was more than a little interested in this girl who had suddenly popped into his life. He had been wary of females since Elaine, but this one seemed fresh and unaggressive and he found himself drawn to her. He did not realize how strangely persistent she was being, how she kept leading him back to Elaine and asking questions, masking her insistence with a light touch.

"Yes, I was in love with her," he said. "We had a wild affair going most of that summer and we should have left it at that. She was living out at her beach house then and . . ."

Neil poured himself another brandy he didn't need and looked into the fire without seeing it. All he saw was a gray shingled house on a secluded part of a beach. It was secluded because it was on a private inlet and Elaine's father had bought enough property to insure his privacy while the cost was still within reason.

The house was not elaborate, just a solid frame job with three bedrooms and a bath. What made it attractive was a big living room with mullioned windows overlooking the water and a large sun deck, where he and Elaine had often lain looking at the stars or making love. Her father must be paying huge taxes now, but it seemed to Neil that neither Elaine nor her mother had put much into it through the years.

The furniture was worn, the curtains faded, the beds musty, most of the china chipped and the glasses a mixture of good crystal and jelly jars. Elaine wrote her poetry on a picnic table in the living room, shoving aside dishes and glasses and magazines to make room, or during good weather she stretched out on an old canvas chaise on the sun deck, her sexy body almost naked in her brief bikini, her dark hair blowing in the breeze, her pad on her knees, staring out at the sea or writing furiously. She did not bother much with housework or cooking and slopped around in jeans or the bikini or sometimes nothing, but when she had a modeling appointment in the city, the picture changed like magic.

She would get up in the morning, slip into an old robe and make coffee in the untidy kitchen, her hair dangling, her face colorless, then she would go up to her bedroom and return a half hour later dressed for the city, her hair shining, her make-up perfect, her clothes smart, expensive and becoming.

He had spent entirely too much time with her that summer, neglecting his work to rush out to Westport whenever he got the chance, and, of course, he spent almost every weekend with her. They had started out before the season, when there were few other people around, but even after the city schools closed and families arrived, their privacy was not invaded. There were no houses in the immediate vicinity and with the quick turnover of the beach cottages, there were no old friends of Elaine's or her mother's to intrude.

When some friendly new neighbor called, Elaine would make it clear that she was a poet and did not want to be disturbed at her work. Now and then a happy drunk turned up to invite them to a party in progress, or children came trying to sell them things, but they were all sent away, and when some unsuspecting city people staked out a part of the beach and prepared to settle down for the day, Elaine would stop everything to go and tell them that it was *her* beach and they were trespassing. Their glowering glances as they trudged off with their gear did not faze her.

Nothing did, apparently, but her poetry and their mad affair. They swam and sunbathed and took long walks on the beach and made love. They seemed to be at the height of their passion for each other and Neil had never been happier in his life. He could not make head or tail out of her poems, which seemed allegorical, but since she never tried to sell them she was never disappointed.

They had a few tiffs, but nothing serious. Neil, with his artistic temperament, couldn't understand why she didn't fix up her house or why they ate from cans unless he did the marketing himself, which he did on weekends, but when he tried to change things, he got nowhere. Elaine drifted around, thinking of her verses, or working on them, her dark eyes dreamy, a million miles away from everyday cares.

He had never known she had a temper until he had made a remark about her extravagance. She made very good money modeling and spent almost all of it on clothes, perfume, jewelry, expensive lunches and taxis on the days she went to the city. That she could spend so much on herself and live on canned food and neglect her house shocked him.

"For God's sake, what do you expect me to do?" she had shouted at him. "When I'm out here, that's one thing, but in town I'm competing with the most glamorous women in the world. You don't show up at *Harper's* or *Vogue* in a moth-eaten stole and a dress from Macy's basement."

At the time she had been wearing faded blue jeans that were too tight and an old shirt hanging out over her stomach. He had burst out laughing, but she had not seen the humor. It had turned into a serious argument, the beginning of the end.

Neil felt a light touch on his arm and turned to see Nancy gazing at him expectantly, her head cocked to one side, her fingers stroking her temple, shoving back her hair, a gesture he had seen Elaine use hundreds of times.

"Come back to me," Nancy said with a wry little smile. "You left me dangling."

"Let's forget it. Would you like another brandy?"

"Thanks, I still have some."

Mrs. Mallory came in to ask if there was anything she could do before she retired, and then withdrew. They sat there silently for a while, Neil wishing he had never laid eyes on Elaine Parker and Nancy sipping the last of her brandy thoughtfully. It was only then that he realized how persistent she had been, how many questions she had asked and how she kept leading the conversation back to Elaine.

"Why are you so damned interested in Elaine?" he asked.

Nancy looked startled. "I told you. I'm trying to find her. That friend of hers I told you about is worried about her."

"Why ask me?" Neil asked defensively. "I told you I haven't seen her for over a year."

"That's what seems queer."

"What does?"

"I've talked to several of her friends and none of them has seen or heard of her since the week after she closed the beach house. They all seem to think she left New York, but nobody knows where she went or where she is now. Doesn't that seem strange to you?"

"Frankly, I don't give a damn where she is."

The phone in the den rang just then and he crossed the room to answer it.

Kate Vail's voice came over the line. He had told her he had invited Nancy to dine with him when he had said his good-bys earlier and now she said she hoped she wasn't interrupting anything.

"Oh, no," he said. "We were just talking."

"I wouldn't have called this late, but you left your brief case and I was afraid you wouldn't know where to look for it. I can send it over to your office in the morn . . . Oh, no, tomorrow's Saturday."

"Never mind, Kate. I'll pick it up over the weekend, but thanks for calling."

"Having fun?" Kate's low voice sounded amused. "Nancy's a pretty little thing, isn't she? So different from Elaine, you'd never know they were cousins."

"*Cousins?*"

"Didn't she tell you?"

Neil glared at a landscape over the den fireplace. "No, she didn't."

"Well, her mother is George Parker's sister and you must know that George is Elaine's father. He's retired now and living out in Phoenix. Arthritis, poor man. He can't get around much any more. Let me know when you're coming and I'll buy you a drink."

There was a click and he was left holding the dead phone, staring at it as though it had bitten him. He was astonished for a moment or two, then puzzled and finally furious. He slammed down the receiver and returned to the living room, his tall body stiff and formal, his blue eyes blazing.

Nancy looked at him over the back of the sofa and her glance followed him as he circled around it and stood in front of her.

"That was Kate Vail," he said angrily. "Why in hell didn't you tell me you're Elaine's cousin? You deliberately gave me the impression you barely knew her. Why?"

She colored slightly and fingered her bracelet. "Please sit down. You're making me nervous standing there like that."

He flung himself down on the sofa. "There isn't any old friend, is there? Who really sent you to pry into my affairs?"

"Elaine's father," Nancy said uneasily. "He's out in Phoenix and can't come East. I haven't seen him in years, but when my mother wrote him that I was coming to New York, he asked me to look up Elaine. He said he hadn't heard anything from her since she left California and he was worried."

Neil's eyebrows went up. "It took him all that time to start worrying? Over a year and a half?"

Nancy nodded. "It sounds crazy, but they were never close. Uncle George fell for another woman when Elaine was very young and he pulled out. He was very fair about it. Paid Aunt Betsy alimony and child support and gave them that beach house you talked about."

She looked into the fire and brushed aside her bangs. "I used to visit there when I was a kid. I thought Elaine was terrific. She's four years older than I am and I used to copy everything she did. But she was a little strange. She wrote nutty poetry and didn't care much for anything else, except boys and dates, of course."

"I got the idea she hated her father. She hardly ever mentioned him."

"I suppose you can't blame her," Nancy said. "He married again and had another family and seemed to forget her. After her mother died and the alimony stopped, she was on her own and I don't think she saw much of him. She was very bitter about the way he treated her mother. My mother tried to keep in touch with her, but it wasn't easy. She was a very successful fashion model here in New York, but she would get bored and go off on long trips. She lived in the Village for a while and Mexico and a lot of places before she went out to California. We never heard from her except a note now and then or a Christmas card. She never wrote to her father at all unless she wanted something, or so he says."

"Then why his sudden interest after all these years?"

"He's getting old and he's not well. His second wife is dead and his two sons are in college. I suppose he's lonely and wants to patch things up with her. He only knew she was in New York because Andrew Crawford had to get in touch with him about the beach house when she came back from California." Nancy's eyes rested on him. "That must have been about the time you met her."

He nodded impatiently.

"Don't you have any idea where she could be?" Nancy persisted.

"If you've been snooping around for the past week, you must know that I would be the last person who would know." Neil's handsome face hardened. "Or didn't anyone tell you she thinks I tried to kill her?"

She regarded him levelly. "Yes, I heard. That's why I wanted to talk to you. I was afraid that if I told you who I was, you wouldn't want to talk to me. Did you really try to kill her?"

"No, but she went around telling everybody who'd listen that I did," he said wearily. "She damned near ruined me."

"But why?" Nancy asked. "Why would she tell people a dreadful thing like that?"

Neil's irritation increased. "Because she believed it, I guess. I've never really known."

"Is that why she broke off the engagement?"

"Look, Nancy," he said, his voice rising. "Can't you understand that I don't want to talk about Elaine. It took me a long time to get over the thing and I don't give a damn whether she's dead or alive."

Nancy stared at him. "What a horrible thing to say about a woman you once loved."

He poured himself another brandy, drank half of it and regarded his guest with eyes too bright with anger and liquor.

"Elaine might be your cousin, but she's the worst bitch I ever met in my life," he said.

"Then why in hell did you ask her to marry you?"

"I told you I don't want to talk about it."

She reached out and touched his hand. "Please tell me about it," she said gently. "So far I've only heard what Elaine's friends had to say, and they seem biased."

Their eyes met and he suddenly realized that for the first time he wanted to tell someone his side of it, but it wouldn't be easy. His emotions were still too strong. He lit a cigarette and wondered where to begin.

"We didn't discuss marriage in the beginning," he said, finally. "I had no money and no prospects then, but Elaine seemed to think we would get married and I let her think so. I even began to think that we could muddle through somehow, but then I saw how extravagant she was and that she spent every cent she could get her hands on for clothes and things for herself, never for her home or anything constructive."

He took another swig of his brandy and squinted at the glass, his mind on the past. "I had been brought up by Nellie, who would never spend a dime she could save or stand the sight of a dirty dish in a sink and I began to see that if we got married it would be a disaster. Things came to a head one night when I criticized her extravagance. She got furious and spent the night in one of the guest rooms. I saw the writing on the wall then and . . ."

He noticed that Nancy was leaning back, her eyes closed. "Am I boring you?"

Her eyes flew open. "No. I'm just trying to get the picture. It's been so long since I've seen Elaine."

A log broke and sent embers out onto the hearth. Neil got up and swept them back into the fire, put on another log and returned to the sofa again, rubbing his forehead with his fingertips.

"That night was one of the worst in my life," he went on. "I was mad about Elaine, insane about her, but I couldn't face the prospect of spending the rest of my life in debt or fighting about money. It almost killed me, but I decided that the next morning I would tell her that I could never marry her."

Nancy wasn't leaning back now, she had turned toward him and was looking at him with a puzzled frown. "But I thought she . . ."

"When I told Elaine the next morning, she told me she was pregnant," he said, his voice husky with emotion.

"My God!" Nancy looked shocked. "Is that how you got engaged?"

"Yes."

He probably shouldn't be telling her all this, he thought, but he liked her more than any woman he had met since Elaine and he didn't want to start off with the past between them.

"Elaine wanted a big wedding," he went on doggedly, "but before things were really set, my grandmother got sick and at her age anything could be serious. I was afraid there would be huge medical bills and I was worried about them. I didn't let Nellie know, of course, but I asked Elaine if we could put off the wedding until we knew how things would turn out."

Nancy reached for a cigarette, lit it before he could, and blew out a little cloud of smoke. "If I knew Elaine, she refused," she said. "She always raised hell if she didn't get her own way."

He nodded. "She refused flatly. That was on a Friday and I spent the weekend worrying about it, then on Sunday afternoon, when Elaine was out, I phoned the hospital and they told me Nellie was worse. I didn't tell Elaine then, but waited until late that night, when she seemed in a mellow mood. It was a lovely moonlight night and we were out on the sun deck drinking wine coolers. It took me a long time to get up the courage to mention it again, but I . . ." His voice trailed off and he took another sip of his brandy.

"Go on," Nancy urged. "What did you say?"

"I told her that I didn't see how we could afford to have the baby. She would have to give up modeling and I was barely making enough to keep my office going and with Nellie . . ." He paused again, twirling his glass, obviously embarrassed. "I asked her if she would have an abortion."

He blurted it out, his face flushed and his eyes sad and angry; then he turned to Nancy. "Have I shocked you?"

She shook her head. "I can't think of anything worse than having a child you don't want or can't support. How did Elaine take it?"

"She had a fit. She said it was too late and I was asking her to risk her life because I was a selfish bastard. I was a monster who had gotten her pregnant and then wanted to get rid of her and her baby. It was awful. She started screaming that she would never have an abortion and nobody on earth could make her. It was murder. It went on and on."

Neil looked into the past again, seeing Elaine's beautiful face contorted with rage. "I tried to reason with her, but I couldn't, so I finally gave up and went into the house. She ran down to the beach and stalked off in the moonlight. She always did that when she was upset."

"Did you go after her?"

"No, there was never any point in trying to discuss anything with her when she was angry. I thought I'd talk to her again in the morning, when she had calmed down, and then I went to bed."

He reached for the brandy, held up the bottle and looked at Nancy. She shook her head and he poured himself another shot, trying to fortify himself against the memory of that hideous night.

"I don't know how long I was asleep, but when I woke up there was a woman down on the beach screaming like mad. I looked out the window and saw Elaine in the moonlight. There was a dock not far from the house and she was sitting on the sand near it, yelling her head off. Before I could get to her, she got up and started to stagger down the beach away from the house.

"I ran after her and when I caught up with her, she turned on me like a wild cat. She was soaking wet and I had a hard time holding her. She kept screaming that I had tried to kill her and pulling away from me."

"It sounds crazy," Nancy said. "Was she on pot or something?"

Neil shook his head. "She didn't even smoke cigarettes. That's what made it so terrible. She honestly seemed to think I'd tried to murder her. When I finally dragged her to the house and put her on the sofa, she looked as though she were scared to death of me."

Nancy looked puzzled, but said nothing.

"I managed to get a shot of whiskey down her and a blanket over her while she cringed on the sofa as though I might strangle her at any moment."

"What did you think?" Nancy asked.

"I thought her mind had snapped or perhaps she had been crazy all along and I never knew it, so I was very gentle and firm with her. She finally told me she had walked up the beach for a while, then, instead of coming back to the house, she had gone to sit on the dock because she was still furious. She swore I had come up behind her, pushed her into the water and held her down, trying to drown her. She said she stopped struggling so I would think she was dead and let go."

The memory of that last, horrible night rose in his mind like an evil dream. Elaine huddled on the sofa, her wet hair hanging down around her face, her dark eyes smoldering with fear and hatred, her voice harsh as she made her accusations.

"She said she faked it until I let her go, then got under the dock and waited until she heard me running on top of it, then she got as far as the beach and passed out. When she came to she started to scream."

Nancy frowned. "Could someone else have done it?"

He smiled skeptically. "When I heard the screaming and turned on the light it was almost three. Can you imagine someone just happening to walk by at three o'clock in the morning, seeing Elaine on the dock and deciding to drown her? Besides, there wasn't a soul around. There never was late at night. Most of the summer people had kids and turned in fairly early, particularly on Sundays."

Neil got up, went over to the fireplace and leaned against the mantel. He was wearing a gray tweed suit and the rain had made his dark hair try to curl. He ran his fingers through it, mussing it more.

"I pointed out that I was wearing pajama bottoms and they were dry except for the damp places where I had come in contact with her. That didn't help at all. She said I hadn't been in the water, but shoved her off the dock and held her down with my arms. She thought I must have lain flat and it was high tide and even if I had gotten wet, I'd have had time to change."

Nancy looked at him, her glance very direct. "Then you think she honestly believed you had tried to kill her?"

He nodded miserably. "She even told people that when I shoved her off the dock I yelled, 'Goddamn it, I'm never going to marry you.'"

Returning to the sofa, he lit another cigarette and forced himself to go on. "It was like a nightmare. She waited until I went to make some coffee, then ran upstairs to the bathroom and locked herself in. I tried to talk to her through the door, but she kept screaming that I was a homicidal maniac and she never wanted to see me again."

Neil's voice became bitter. "She never did. I packed up my things and walked to the station. It took me the rest of the night and I never saw her or the beach house again."

"She never reported it to the police or anything?"

He scowled and drew on his cigarette. "I thought she might, but she didn't. Instead, she went back to the city and started talking. She never told anyone she was pregnant, but she told all our friends that I was a maniac who had tried to kill her and that I should be locked up."

"Did they believe her?"

"I don't know, but I understand she was very convincing. When anyone questioned her about me, or tried to take my side, she said that if I denied it, I was lying or insane and didn't know I had done it. I've heard of cases like that."

"That's a very serious charge," Nancy said gravely. "She must have known that."

He nodded again. "She really laid it on. She was afraid to stay at her beach house alone after what had happened and was so terrified of me she was going to close it and go away. The inference being that I would try again, I suppose. Anyway, she did close the house and I heard she was at some hotel here in town, but that's the last I heard. Maybe she went back to the Coast."

He studied the tip of his cigarette, still scowling. "For a while I noticed people looking at me as though they were wondering if the story were true, and several girls I asked for dates put me off politely, but I've never really known if any of them believed it. I do know that I wasn't invited out as much as I had been before I knew Elaine, and things might have gotten worse, but Nellie died not long afterwards and I got all that money and I was suddenly in again." He laughed a little harshly. "Strange what money can do."

They sat in silence for several minutes; then Neil smiled thinly. "Well, you wanted the truth and now you've got it. Pretty, isn't it?"

Nancy was giving him another of her direct gazes. "What did you intend to do?"

"About what?" he asked, surprised.

"Were you going ahead and marry her if she wouldn't have an abortion, or walk away from the whole thing?"

"I don't really know." He frowned. "I never had time to think it over. I went to bed that night, as I told you, and the next thing I knew she was accusing me of attempted murder and then she kicked me out. I didn't have time to . . ."

He broke off, suddenly aware that Nancy's eyes were no longer friendly and interested. They were cool and rather scornful.

"And you tell me you don't care where Elaine is or what happened to her?" she asked.

"You're damned right," he said angrily. "I just hope I never lay eyes on her again."

Now Nancy did look shocked. "But, my God, Neil, she was pregnant with your child. Didn't you ever worry about that? Didn't you ever wonder . . . ?"

"I gave up worrying about Elaine a long time ago and

I'm not going to start again now," he said flatly. "As far as I am concerned, she's dead."

She studied him with an odd expression, as though he were an old painting that might be a fake; then she glanced at her watch and got up. "I really must be leaving. It's getting late."

He got up too, a little drunk by then and annoyed at the tack she had suddenly taken. "I'll call down for a cab and see you home," he said stiffly. "Where is it?"

She mentioned an apartment hotel on lower Fifth Avenue, then hastily added, "But you don't have to go with me. I'll be all right."

His lips turned up in a mirthless smile. "Afraid I'll strangle you in the cab?"

"Don't be an idiot."

He got her things for her and escorted her to the foyer, where he rang for the elevator. She seemed strangely quiet and thoughtful standing there waiting, and he wondered if he had been a fool to tell her the truth.

"You think I'm a heel, don't you?" he asked.

She looked up at him and brushed her light brown bangs aside, her expression still cool.

"Let's just say that I can understand how you feel about Elaine, but I don't see how you can be so callous about your baby. You don't even know . . ."

His eyes were suddenly blazing. "There wasn't a damn thing I could do about it, can't you see that? I couldn't have gotten within a mile of her if I'd wanted to. I had to put her out of my mind or go crazy, and the baby was part of her."

Nancy backed up, a little frightened by his temper.

"I suppose you're right," she said. "Anyway, thanks for telling me the truth. I appreciate it."

"Humoring me?" he asked acidly.

The elevator arrived then and Nancy graciously thanked him for a lovely evening before the elevator swallowed her up. He stood there in the foyer for a moment or two, smelling a trace of her delicate perfume; then he swore and went back to the living room, a savage expression on his handsome face.

He was thinking of Elaine and wondering if he would ever get over the memory of her.

∌⋉⋊∋

Nancy's apartment, a living room, bedroom and small kitchen, seemed drab after Neil's lovely penthouse, but it was adequate and she didn't mind the hotel-furniture look, because she was already looking for an apartment of her own. She was also looking for a job, something to do with words, she hoped, like newspaper or magazine work.

She put her damp stole away, then collapsed on the dun-colored sofa and lit a cigarette. Although it was well after midnight, it would be two hours earlier in Phoenix and Uncle George would be waiting for her call. She was not worried about that. What worried her was how much to tell him. She had told him the night before that Kate Vail was having a party where she would be likely to meet the man Elaine had been engaged to.

Nancy had already told him about the rumors she had heard and promised to get Neil Stratton's version of the affair if she could, and report it to him. Well, now she had it, but should she edit it? George Parker had a bad heart along with his arthritis and the news might throw him. But he was also a tough old bird who had been around for sixty-five years and survived most of them in business and probably not much could shock him now. She picked up the phone and dialed.

The last time she had seen her uncle he'd had gray at his temples and a pepper and salt mustache. Now they were probably white and his strong body wouldn't be the same, but the classical features he had handed down to Elaine would have stayed with him and she visualized him as looking distinguished. His voice was still vigorous as it came over the line, eager for her news.

"Well, it's not too pleasant," she said. "In fact, it's a little sordid."

"Never mind that. I want the truth, but first tell me about this Neil Stratton. What kind of a guy is he?"

"Tall, well dressed, about twenty-six or -seven and quite handsome. Very blue eyes that seem to look right through you. His grandmother was a cook, but if he were an actor, he could play the part of an Irish duke."

"I don't mean his looks, I mean the *man*. Anything queer about him? Did he seem normal?"

Nancy took a drag on her cigarette and frowned. "He seemed very intense about things, but that could be because he hated talking about Elaine. He hardly smiled at all, except at dinner, when he was talking about planning villages and landscaping."

"What did he say about Elaine?"

She told him, trying to remember every detail she could and not coloring anything. When she had finished, Uncle George seemed stunned. There was a dead silence on his end of the wire.

"What worries me is the child," Nancy said, "but that didn't seem to bother him at all."

"I wouldn't worry about that," Uncle George said, finally.

"Why not?"

"I don't think there is one." There was another long pause. "I think Elaine either had an abortion or she's dead."

Nancy gasped and held the phone tighter. "Why do you think that?"

"If she was in her right mind, she'd never have had a child by a man she thought was a homicidal maniac, and if she'd had it, how could she have lived? She didn't try to sell the beach house or even rent it. I've checked on that. It is still closed just as she left it."

"Maybe she had some money Neil didn't know about, or some friends she could go to. Remember she told him she thought an abortion was murder."

"That was before the alleged attack." Uncle George was silent again and she could hear his heavy breathing.

"Are you all right, Uncle George?"

"Yes, but I'm very worried. When a pregnant woman refuses to get rid of a child its father doesn't want and then disappears, there has to be something wrong. I'd like to know more about this Stratton guy."

Nancy snubbed out her cigarette and was surprised to find herself thinking of those piercing, dark-fringed blue eyes looking at her with a strange mixture of anger, sadness and defiance.

"Uncle George . . ."

"Yes?"

"When you said you thought Elaine might be dead, did you mean murdered?"

"Well, she has gone off for long periods of time before without keeping in touch, but when you add this pregnancy business and the rest of it, the whole thing begins to smell."

"But, Uncle George, Elaine went around telling everybody that Neil had tried to kill her, but she never told anyone that she was pregnant by him."

"It's hardly something she'd boast about, is it?"

"You seem to be saying that he might have killed her because she was pregnant and he wanted to get rid of her."

"I'm not saying that. I'm just saying that it seems possible."

Nancy's forehead wrinkled. "If that were the case, then why on earth would he tell me about it? No one else knew she was pregnant."

"Damned if I know, unless he felt some compulsion . . .

Tell me, Nancy, did he seem to be telling the truth when he denied having attacked her that night?"

She thought about it. The last thing she wanted to do was defend a man who might have murdered her cousin and gotten away with it, but she wanted to be fair, too. "Yes, he did, but . . ." Her voice trailed off.

"You're thinking that Elaine might have been right when she said he could be insane and not known he had done it. Is that what's bothering you?"

"Yes." Nancy's frown deepened. "But that would make him a weirdo, a creep with a split personality or something, and he didn't seem that way at all. He seemed clean-cut and sensitive and honest. He got a little drunk, but I think it was because talking about Elaine disturbed him. He seems to have gone through hell with her."

"And he's rich and handsome and you liked him," Uncle George cut in. "Think that could sway your judgment?"

"No, of course not," Nancy said, but she did not tell her uncle that Neil's looks and money were not the only things she found attractive about him. There had been some physical magnetism she had felt from the first moment she had seen him. If it had not been for Elaine, she would be in a rosy glow now, thinking that at last she had found a man . . .

"Are you still there, Nancy?"

"Yes, Uncle George. What were you saying?"

"I asked you if you thought it possible that Elaine imagined the attack. She's always had a wild imagination. All that crazy poetry. Even as a child I never understood her. Grasping and determined to get her own way one minute, and off in a cloud the next. What do you think?"

"I don't know, but Neil said she was soaking wet and seemed really terrified of him, then she told everybody she was going as far away from him as she could get." Nancy stopped short as a new thought struck her. "Uncle George, I wonder if we're not getting the wind up over nothing."

"What do you mean?"

"Elaine might be perfectly all right, but if something has happened to her, why should you suspect Neil? Pregnant or not, she was clearing out."

Nancy suddenly felt happier than she had all evening. "He wouldn't have had to kill her to get rid of her. She was getting away from him as fast as she could."

Uncle George let that pass. "Do you know where she stayed after she left the beach house?"

"Kate Vail thought it was the Drake and that she stayed about a week, but it was over a year ago and she wasn't sure. Do you want me to check on it?"

Her uncle seemed to ponder the point for several minutes, then said, "No, dear. I've taken up enough of your time when you've just got back and must have a million things to do getting settled."

His abrupt change surprised Nancy. She had talked to him almost every night since her return and she had spent a good deal of time and energy tracking down Elaine's friends and getting what information she could because he had seemed so worried.

"Are you just going to drop it then?" she asked.

"I think so, but if you should hear anything, let me know, won't you?"

"Yes, of course, but I don't understand. You seemed so worried about Elaine and now . . ."

"I've probably been making mountains out of molehills," Uncle George said with a sigh. "She'll probably turn up one of these days and be furious with us for probing into her affairs. I shouldn't have bothered you with it."

"But, Uncle George . . ."

"Thanks for everything, dear, and give my love to your mother when you write."

The line went dead, but Nancy kept her fingers on the receiver, wondering if she should call him back and ask him for an explanation of his odd behavior. Why should he have gotten her involved with his damned daughter and made a big thing of her disappearance, then suddenly dropped it like a hot brick?

She went to bed angry, thinking that since her teen-age crush she had never really liked her cousin much anyway.

The hell with Elaine.

※

When Neil dropped by the Vails' apartment late the next afternoon to pick up his brief case, he found Kate and Oliver alone for once, because they were going out to dinner and the theater with friends. The servants had the evening off and Oliver let him in. He was a thickset man with a darkish complexion and crisp black hair, sprinkled with silver. His features were a little battered from college boxing and an overly active social life, but there was an engaging warmth about him. He was wearing a maroon dinner jacket and carrying a huge highball when he opened the door.

"You're just in time for a drink," he said, smiling broadly. "Kate's dressing, but she'll be here in a minute."

The apartment seemed huge and empty and strangely quiet after the festivities of the evening before. Neil followed Oliver to the bar which was built into one corner of the living room.

"I just came to get my brief case," he said. "I don't want to hold you up."

But Oliver was already behind the bar. "Nonsense," he said heartily. "Always time for a drink. What'll it be, scotch?"

"Yes, thanks."

Neil sat on a barstool and lit a cigarette.

"Kate said you wound up with Nancy Gilbert last night," Oliver said, busy with ice and bottles. "You'd never dream she was Elaine's cousin, would you? Nothing alike at all."

Kate swept in, looking very smart in a black dinner dress. She was a tall woman and wore her clothes beautifully and even at forty, she had a bouncing vitality.

"Cousins never look alike," she said, flashing her white smile. "I have one who looks like a Pekinese."

She sat at the bar beside Neil and held out an unlit cigarette. "You don't look too well, dear. Anything wrong?"

He had spent a wretched night and awakened with a hangover, but it was worry that really had him down. He bitterly regretted having told Nancy the truth about Elaine and himself. But he said he was fine and lit Kate's cigarette.

She leaned over to get the light, then glanced up at him.

"Trouble with Nancy last night?" she asked in her maternal way. "I thought she would be fun."

"She spent the whole damned evening talking about Elaine," he said. "Why didn't you tell me they were cousins when you introduced us?"

"But I did tell you." Kate turned to her husband. "Make mine light, darling. You know the blasts we'll get at the Fishers'."

Neil picked up the glass Oliver had just put in front of him and frowned at Kate. "Did you know that she had been commissioned by Elaine's father to check up on me?"

Kate dropped a hot ash on her skirt, hurriedly brushed it off and shook her head. "Nancy just told me she was George Parker's niece and that he was worried about Elaine. George and my father were in college together, you know. I simply told Nancy you had been engaged to Elaine and she wanted to meet you."

She spoke quickly, obviously embarrassed. She and Oliver

had been careful not to mention Elaine Parker in front of
Neil since their brief engagement had ended so bitterly.

"I'm sorry if Nancy bothered you, dear," Kate went on,
"but she said her uncle was really worried and . . ."

"*Now* he's worried," Oliver cut in. "Hell, the kid's been
batting around alone for years and now he cares . . ."

"She's no kid." Kate's pleasant voice was a little hard. "I
don't think she ever was a kid."

"Well, I don't quite see why the old bastard's worried
now," Oliver said, wielding his bar rag like a professional.
"She's been going her own way for a long time."

Neil took a long drag on his cigarette, still frowning.

"Nancy had heard Elaine's story of my trying to kill her,"
he said. "She came right out and asked me if it was true."

There was a dead silence; then Kate put her hand on
Neil's arm and gave it a little squeeze. "For heaven's sake,
Neil, don't bring that up again. Nobody believed Elaine.
You know that."

He didn't know that. He had even wondered at the time
if the Vails would have remained loyal to him if Nellie had
not died when she did and left him so much money. And
then, of course, Kate's father still handled the properties
and investments he had inherited.

"Well, it isn't the first time Elaine's gone off on her own,"
Oliver said. "She'll turn up when she feels like it. She always
does. George should realize that. Another drink, Neil?"

"No, thanks. I have to be going."

Oliver gave him his brief case, saw him out, then returned
to the bar and picked up his drink. "Damned shame Nancy
Gilbert had to show up," he said. "It took Neil months to
get over that thing with Elaine and now Nancy's stirred it
all up again."

Kate sat silently for a while, her dark eyes thoughtful;
then she put down her glass. "Oliver, do you think anything
could have happened to Elaine?"

He stared at her across the bar. "What on earth do you mean?"

"Well, I hadn't given it too much thought until Nancy started asking questions, but there does seem something queer about the way she left town. Nobody saw her off and she didn't tell anybody where she was going." Kate looked doubtful. "We usually get a Christmas card from her, but we didn't last year."

Oliver shrugged. "So what? She told everybody she knew that she was going to get as far away from Neil as she could, didn't she?"

Kate nodded.

"She also said she didn't want anybody to know where she was going for fear he would find her." Oliver went on, splashing a short shot into his glass. "So why would she send out Christmas cards?"

"Oh, I don't know, but it does seem a little strange."

"Nonsense, darling. She's probably shacked up with some other guy." He laughed. "Maybe she even married some poor slob."

"You might be right."

"Sure I am. She's the kind of a woman who couldn't spend a week without a man."

"And just how do you know that?" Kate asked.

He leaned over the bar and kissed the top of her head. "I'm psychic," he said, and laughed again.

But Kate merely smiled.

⁂

Sunday turned out to be sunny, hazy and warm. Neil got up late, made himself some coffee and carried it out to the terrace. Mrs. Mallory had Sundays off and had probably gone out to Queens to visit her daughter, as she usually did.

Her cat, a gray Persian named Mike because of his puggish face, escorted Neil to a table under a gay garden umbrella, then sat on the grass and stared at him with round, new-penny eyes.

Neil grinned at him. "Don't hand me that starving bit. I know you've had breakfast."

Mike answered with a pathetic, silent Meow. Neil poured some cream into his saucer and put it down. Mike fell to as though he hadn't had a mouthful in weeks. While Neil drank his coffee, he surveyed the gardens which edged the large turfed terrace.

The mums were at their best, brilliant yellows and bronzes and russets, planned for the fall coloring he missed in the city. The terrace was on the southeast corner of the building, separated from his neighbors by whitewashed brick walls, and he had planted boxwood hedges to hide the guard railings on the outside.

Standing, he could see the East River and to the south, the Pan Am building and the towering office buildings around Grand Central, but sitting, the terrace was arranged to seem like a country garden with small trees and shrubs and pebbled walks. At the far end was a little pool with a fountain in the middle and all around were groups of out-door furniture, carefully planned for parties on summer evenings or lounging around on sunny days.

He would work on the Moncrief plans this morning, he thought, trim the boxwood and clean up the gardens in the afternoon. He had been invited to a buffet at the Temples' that evening, but had called it off, because they were friends of Elaine's as well as his and he did not feel up to a party anyway. He'd had another bad night, his mind reeling back to the past, while he fought desperately to control it, trying to blank out pictures of Elaine that kept appearing, like some awful movie he couldn't turn off.

Work, hard work, was the only solution, he thought. It

had saved his sanity when he and Elaine had broken up and it would again. He made another pot of coffee and shut himself in the den with the Moncrief plans for the rest of the morning. When he emerged for lunch, the house phone was ringing. He answered it, frowning, annoyed at being disturbed, and his frown deepened when the doorman announced Miss Gilbert.

He hesitated, torn between his desire to see Nancy again and his decision not to. She had opened old wounds and if he were fool enough to see her, she would probe deeper, keeping them open and bleeding.

"She says it's important, sir," the doorman said.

"All right, Ned, ask her to come up, please."

He was waiting in the foyer when the elevator doors opened and Nancy stepped out, looking very pretty in a lightweight beige suit. She was smiling but her eyes were serious.

"I'm sorry to bust in on you like this," she said, "but I had to talk to you. I hope you don't mind."

"Not at all," he lied. "Come in."

He led her to the living room, where the french doors were open, giving a full view of the garden beyond.

"Oh, it's beautiful," Nancy said, walking out into the hazy sunshine. "What lovely mums."

"I was just about to have lunch," Neil said. "Mrs. Mallory left some shrimp salad. Like to join me?"

"No, thanks. I have an appointment to look at an apartment in a few minutes. It's just a couple of blocks east of here, so I thought I'd drop by instead of calling."

She settled down on a chaise and lit a cigarette. The sunlight turned her light brown hair to bronze and a gentle breeze from the East River ruffled it. When she looked up at him, he noticed that her eyes seemed more green than blue in the daylight and there was a faint trace of freckles across her short nose.

The Hell with Elaine 39

"What's so important?" he asked, pulling up another chaise.

"I came to apologize for the way I acted the other night." She pushed her bangs aside and gave him a tentative smile. "I had no business prying into your affairs and I'm sorry."

His piercing eyes met hers steadily. "What changed your mind?"

"Well, I was doing it because Uncle George seemed so worried about Elaine, but when I talked to him after I left here Friday night, he said he'd probably been making mountains out of molehills, and dropped the whole thing."

"That seems strange."

"I thought so too, but I'm glad he wants to forget it. I hated all that snooping around and questioning people." She smiled again and this time it wasn't tentative. "Can you forgive me if I promise never to mention Elaine again?"

He smiled too and, reaching out, took her small hand in his.

"I certainly can."

The drone of the traffic on Fifth Avenue was almost inaudible and they could have been sitting in a quiet country garden. Neither of them spoke for a while. A boat on the river hooted and the little fountain babbled merrily.

"What about having dinner with me tonight?" he asked. "Mrs. Mallory isn't here today, but we could go over to Luigi's. It's a little place over on Third I often go to."

"I'd love to." Nancy looked at her watch. "Woops, I've got to run."

"Shall I pick you up around six?"

"No. I have two more apartments to look at, then a cocktail party. I'll meet you at Luigi's. Where is it exactly?"

He told her and went to the foyer with her. While they waited for the elevator, he kissed her lightly.

"I can't tell you how glad I am you came," he said. "I had thought it might be better if I didn't see you again."

She wrinkled her nose in a cute way. "I was afraid of that."

He kissed her again before the elevator came and this time she responded. It was nothing like Elaine's animal eagerness, but a tender, sweet response that entranced him.

"See you later, darling," he said, and watched the doors close behind her.

He went to fix lunch, thinking how wonderful it was to say that to a woman again. He'd had a lot of dates and a few halfhearted affairs since Elaine, but none of them had given him any pleasure. He was terrified of getting another woman pregnant and he didn't trust the Pill, because he no longer trusted women, so his affairs had been disappointing and the dates boring. But Nancy was different. He felt sure he could trust her.

After all, she was nothing like Elaine.

✦

The next morning Neil had to drive out to Connecticut again, this time to a large nursery in Ridgefield, where he spent most of the day tagging trees and shrubs for the Moncrief job, and it was late in the afternoon when he got to his office. Harriet Hart, the trim middle-aged receptionist he had acquired when he became Allen Rutland's partner, greeted him with a warm smile.

"Mr. Robert Ewing has called three times, Mr. Stratton," she said, looking up from her typewriter. "And Mr. Rutland wants to see you. There's some complication on the North Carolina job."

Neil nodded and went down the hall to Allen's office, where he found his partner leaning over a worktable, studying a layout of blueprints. They were plans for a new resort hotel in Ashville.

"Sorry to be so late," Neil said. "I got tied up at Woodcock's."

Allen Rutland was a tall, slim man in his early forties with thinning brown hair and a long, pleasant face. He lived in Eastchester with his wife and two young daughters. Although they had only been partners for a year, they had known each other for a long time, since Cornell, when Allen spent a term teaching there and Neil had been one of his students.

"Seems we're going to have some trouble with the grading," Allen said, pointing to the blueprints with the stem of his pipe. "The way they've got it, they'll drown anything we plant along this south line to screen the street."

Neil looked at the blueprints, and Allen, watching him, noticed that for the first time in almost a year, his young partner seemed happy. He was wearing slacks and a sports jacket and had acquired a slight tan while visiting nurseries during the past week. But more important, there seemed to be a trace of the old twinkle in Neil's eyes and some of the gaiety he had lost.

"Find gold in Connecticut or is it a new girl?" Allen asked, grinning.

Neil straightened up and grinned back at his partner. "A girl. A wonderful. Her name is Nancy Gilbert." He hesitated and then added, "She's Elaine Parker's cousin."

Allen stiffened and his grin died. "You must be a glutton for punishment," he said.

He had met Elaine and disliked her and he knew of the accusations she had spread all over town later. He had also watched his partner come close to a breakdown and slowly pull himself out of it. The phone rang, saving him from saying something rude. He crossed to his desk, picked up the receiver, then turned to Neil.

"It's for you," he said.

Neil took the receiver and heard Bob Ewing's voice, impatient and a little excited.

"For God's sake, I've been trying to get you all day," he said. "I've got to see you as soon as possible."

"Well, I'm tied up now and I have a date later."

"With Nancy Gilbert?"

"Why, yes. I'm meeting her at the Plaza at six."

"I want to see you before you see her again. I'll meet you at the Oak Room at five-thirty."

"All right." Neil hung up, frowning.

"Something wrong?" Allen asked.

"I don't know."

When he got to the Plaza, he found Bob in the Oak Room contemplating a martini. The huge paneled room was crowded with other men talking business and people meeting for cocktails. There was the usual babble of voices and waiters hurrying with quiet dignity. Neil pulled out a chair and sat down across from Bob. A waiter appeared and he ordered a scotch, then turned to Bob.

"What's on your mind?"

Bob's dark eyes looked very grave behind his glasses and for once he seemed uncertain. He looked at Neil for several seconds, then raised his chin and straightened his tie.

"You know, of course, that Nancy Gilbert is Elaine's cousin?"

"Yes, I know."

"Do you know she's going all over town raking up that trouble you had with Elaine?"

Neil nodded. "Her uncle asked her to try and find Elaine and she tried to, but she's given up on it."

"Given up? Are you crazy? She was at Bobo Babson's cocktail party yesterday with Paul Kendell, that photographer who used to work with Elaine, and of course you know Bobo."

Neil nodded again. Bobo was a tall, thin blonde who looked wonderful in fashion pictures and emaciated in real life. She and Elaine had lived together for a while before Elaine had opened her beach house. Neil had the idea that

Bobo might have believed Elaine's vicious story, and had avoided her.

Bob knocked back his martini and ordered another when the waiter brought Neil's scotch.

"What makes you think she's given up?" he asked.

"She came to my apartment yesterday afternoon and told me so."

"Well, she hasn't," Bob said, scowling at him. "I was there with Carol and I heard her pumping people. I heard her ask Bobo if she remembered when she had last seen Elaine."

Neil stared at him. "*What?*"

"It's true, Neil. I don't give a damn what she told you, but she's doing more than raking up the whole mess, she's making it seem as though there's something sinister about it."

"What do you mean, sinister?" Neil asked, his eyes narrowing.

"Well, by the time Carol and I left, she had everybody talking about Elaine and speculating about where she could be and then, of course, they started off on her story about your trying to kill her."

Bob paused and lit a cigarette and his dark eyes met Neil's.

"I don't think many people took Elaine's story seriously a year ago, but with this they're beginning to talk as though . . . well, as though something might have happened to her. They're saying it's strange nobody has heard from her or seen her in all this time."

Neil looked down at his drink, feeling as though the bottom had dropped out of everything. He thought of Nancy at Luigi's the night before, coming straight to meet him from Bobo's party. They'd had steak Chateaubriand and two bottles of Luigi's best burgundy. Nancy had looked delightful in a gold-colored cocktail dress and her mink stole.

She had told him funny stories about the French and Italian men she had met and he had told her about his dreams of designing an entire new village some day. They had laughed and chatted and he'd had a wonderful evening. They had not once mentioned Elaine.

"Neil, you can't go on seeing Nancy. I don't know what she's up to, but she'll ruin you if she keeps this up." Bob looked grimly businesslike. "There isn't any legal way to shut her up, but perhaps as your lawyer, I could . . ."

Neil shook his head. "It's too late now, Bob," he said, his voice strained. "You're right. I shouldn't have seen her again. I was crazy enough to think . . ."

"Do you want me to meet her for you and tell her you had to leave town or something?"

"No, I want to get out of here. Let's go."

Neil paid their bill and they went out the Fifth Avenue entrance.

"I'm going up to Carol's. Shall we share a cab?" Bob asked as they reached the sidewalk, where a line of taxis waited.

"I think I'll walk," Neil said. "Thanks for warning me about Nancy."

Bob nodded and signaled the first cab in line. Neil stood undecided. He had told Mrs. Mallory that he wouldn't be home for dinner and now it was too late to change plans. He felt like getting drunk, but that wouldn't help anything. He finally crossed Fifty-ninth Street and strode up Fifth Avenue, walking quickly, trying to work off his anger and disappointment.

Without thinking about it, he automatically turned east and a few minutes later was in front of his apartment house. He started to turn in, but changed his mind and kept going. Mrs. Mallory was probably having an early dinner and if he knew women, Nancy might show up to find out why he had not kept their date. He went on, turned north on Third

Avenue and presently was ordering a stiff drink from his favorite waiter at Luigi's.

Antonio was a romantic old boy from Naples and Nancy had charmed him by being able to speak to him in halting Italian.

"The young lady will be coming, yes?" Antonio asked, his dark eyes sparkling.

"No, not tonight."

"Ah, but here she is," Antonio said, glancing toward the door.

Neil turned and saw Nancy stop and look around the room, then spot him and wave. Antonio hurried to her, brought her to the table and seated her with a flourish.

"A very dry martini, per'aps?" he asked, remembering the night before.

Nancy took off her gloves and smiled up at the old waiter.

"*Sì, Antonio, per favore,*" she said.

Antonio went off to the bar at the back of the room. It was early for New York dining and there weren't many people in the restaurant, but there were flowers and candles on each table and the aroma of good food gave it a snug festive air. Soft string music played in the background over the murmur of voices.

Neil turned to Nancy the second Antonio was out of earshot.

"What in hell are you doing here?" he asked.

Her eyes, bright in the candlelight, snapped at him.

"I might ask you the same thing."

He felt his face flush. "It was a mistake seeing you again and I don't intend to repeat it."

Nancy was wearing the little black suit she'd worn when he first met her and her hair was brushed up, giving her a more sophisticated look, but her expression was that of an angry, hurt child.

"I saw you come out of the Plaza with that Ewing man and I followed you. Why did you run out on me?"

She lit a cigarette from the candle and leaned back in her chair, waiting for his answer.

He hesitated, not wanting to bring Bob into it, then realized he couldn't help it.

"You came to my apartment yesterday and told me you were sorry for prying into my affairs, didn't you?"

"Yes."

"And you said your uncle had lost interest and you were dropping the whole thing. Right?"

She nodded.

"Then what in hell were you doing questioning people at Bobo Babson's yesterday afternoon? You lied to me. You haven't dropped it at all. You're still snooping around and trying to make it seem as though there's something fishy about Elaine's disappearance. Bob Ewing heard you." He was angry and had trouble keeping his voice down; then Antonio returned with Nancy's drink, silencing him completely for a few minutes.

"Well?" he said when the waiter had left again.

Nancy's expression had softened and she looked more worried than annoyed.

"I'm afraid there *is* something fishy about it, Neil." She took a sip of her martini. "I honestly meant to drop it, but when Paul asked me to go to a cocktail party with him, I didn't know it would be a den of Elaine's friends. Almost everybody there seemed to know her and they were all talking about her."

"And you know why, don't you?" he asked angrily. "Because you've spent the past week raking into the past and trying to make something of it." He stopped short, frowning. "What did you mean by saying you're afraid something is fishy?"

Nancy leaned forward. "I told you I meant to drop the

whole thing and I meant it, but when Paul and I were in a taxi going up to Bobo's, he asked me if it was true that I was Elaine's cousin, and when I said yes, he said there was something he thought I should know."

She stopped and glanced around the room, as though making sure she would not be overheard. The nearest people were an older couple two tables away and the hidden stereo was playing Mediterranean songs, but she lowered her voice.

"He said that about thirteen months ago, on the morning of August twenty-second, to be exact, he had an appointment to photograph Elaine for a *Vogue* ad. When she didn't turn up, he phoned the Drake, where she had been staying, and they told him she had checked out early that morning. She finally showed up about an hour late and after they finished work, she told him she'd had to leave the hotel because she was broke, and asked him to lend her a thousand dollars."

Nancy paused and took a sip of her drink.

"Go on."

"He is married, but he must have been a little in love with her, because he told her he didn't have that much, but would try to raise it that afternoon. He asked her where she was staying, but she didn't tell him. She just said she would come back at five-thirty."

"Could he raise the money?"

"Yes, he spent the afternoon hitting his friends for it, and had it ready when she came back. She said she was expecting a check soon and would get the money back to him within a week." Nancy snuffed out her cigarette and looked across at Neil, her eyes solemn. "That's the last time he ever saw her."

Neil couldn't see her point. "What's so strange about that? She told everybody she knew that she was leaving town and she couldn't have gotten to Newark without money.

Isn't it obvious? She needed money to get wherever she was going."

"Paul thought that if she really was expecting a check, she would have had to stay somewhere in the city until it came, and it seems that she had borrowed money from him before and always paid it back promptly."

"Why hasn't he told anybody about this before?"

"He and his wife were having trouble and he didn't want her to know about it. She's a buyer for Gimbels and spends every August and September abroad. She's in Europe now. He thought Elaine would pay him back before his wife returned and when she didn't he tried to find her."

"And he couldn't?"

"No. He was afraid to ask too many questions for fear his wife would hear about it, but he got the idea that Elaine might have gone to Bobo Babson's while she was waiting for her check. Bobo denied it, but he thought she might have been lying. She is Elaine's only close friend and Paul thought she might have been trying to hide her."

"From my homicidal mania, no doubt," Neil said grimly.

Nancy blushed and took another sip of her martini. "Paul didn't want to go on about it yesterday, so I cornered Bobo and asked her point-blank when she had last seen Elaine. She was vague. She'd had lunch with Elaine somewhere around that time, but she couldn't remember whether it was before or after the twenty-second. She doesn't keep an engagement book except for business appointments."

Antonio arrived to take their dinner order and Neil, who would not have considered having dinner with Nancy half an hour before, found himself ordering.

When they were alone again, Nancy said, "Doesn't it seem queer to you, Neil? Elaine checks out of the hotel in the morning, gets a thousand from Paul Kendell that afternoon and that's the last anybody has seen or heard of her."

He frowned at her. "Why didn't you tell me all this last

night? You had just come from Bobo's when you met me here."

"I thought you'd be furious if you knew I'd gotten mixed up in it again and I was right. You were furious, and Bob Ewing obviously thinks I'm a meddling bitch." She gave him a sad little smile. "Are you still mad?"

"You probably meant well, but I don't see what good it does to know the exact date Elaine left town. What difference does it make?"

Nancy looked at him steadily for a moment or two. She seemed uncertain, then apparently made a decision.

"Neil, I think you should try to find Elaine."

His head snapped up. "*Me?* Why in hell would I want to find her?"

"I mean, for your own sake, not hers," Nancy said. "And I don't mean you personally, I mean a good detective agency. You can certainly afford it."

Neil laughed harshly. "I should spend good money to find a woman I never want to see again? You've got to be kidding."

"Finding her is the only way to stop all this terrible gossip, Neil. I'm afraid that if you don't do it, someone else will."

He glanced at her sharply. "Who?"

She looked down at the stranded olive in her martini glass.

"The police. If someone reports her missing, they're bound to start digging into it." She raised her eyes to meet his. "It would look a lot better if you beat them to it."

Color rushed to his face and his blue eyes blazed. "You don't believe me, do you? You don't believe that I never saw Elaine after that night at the beach house."

Nancy reached over and took his hand. "Of course, I believe you," she said gently. "It's just what others might believe that is worrying me."

He set his jaw in a stubborn line and said nothing.

"*Please*, darling. All you would have to do is find a good agency and . . ."

Neil carefully lit a cigarette, blew out a cloud of smoke and watched it fade away. "I wouldn't spend a dime to see Elaine dance a jig in hell," he said.

Nancy withdrew her hand. Antonio arrived and began to put dishes in front of them. They made a show of trying to enjoy the food, but neither of them could eat much.

When they left the restaurant and went out to Third Avenue, it was still daylight, but the sun was fading, its last rays hidden by tall buildings. The air was still and getting cooler and people were hurrying home or busy with errands. Neil and Nancy stood outside the little restaurant, she small and grave, he tall, handsome and still angry.

"Are you sure you won't reconsider it?" Nancy asked, looking up at him anxiously.

"Positive," he said, setting his jaw again. "As far as I am concerned, the subject is closed."

Her clear eyes cooled and then hardened.

"I wouldn't be too sure of that," she said, and turned away.

He stood there and watched her disappear in the crowd of hurrying pedestrians. If only she could mind her own business, he thought, things would have been so different. Now she seemed to have joined the enemy camp, the people who thought that he had tried to get rid of Elaine and perhaps succeeded.

"The hell with them all," he muttered to himself, and went home to spend another restless night.

⊱❦⊰

Neil spent the next day at the Moncrief job up in Westchester and did not get to his office at all, but when he arrived on Wednesday morning he had barely settled down to work when Allen Rutland came in, his expression grave. He sat on the edge of Neil's desk and re-lit his pipe, studying his partner over the flame of a match.

"Are you in any kind of trouble, Neil?" he asked finally, waving out the match.

Neil smiled. "No more than usual, I hope. Why?"

"There was a man here yesterday. Said his name was Sam Turner, and that he had a landscaping job in New Jersey to be done and wanted to talk to you about it."

"What's wrong with that?" Neil asked, leaning back in his chair.

"There was something queer about it," Allen said. "Harriet said a man had called earlier and she told him you wouldn't be in until this morning. He hung up without leaving his name, then about an hour later this Sam Turner showed up asking for you. From his voice, Harriet was sure he was the same man who had called, but he didn't mention it. She told him you wouldn't be in until today and asked if he wanted to see me instead."

"Did he?"

Allen nodded. "He told me he had bought a small factory in East Orange and wanted to have it landscaped. We talked about it for a while and then he began asking questions about you. How long I had known you, what kind of a man were you and stuff like that. When I balked, he went back to talking about the job. He said his firm made garden furniture, so it was important that the landscaping be good."

"What was the name of his firm?"

"Garden Comfort." Allen frowned and ran his hand over his thinning hair. "I had Harriet check after he left and there's no such place in East Orange."

Neil got up and went to the window, where he looked down at the busy traffic and scurrying people on the street below. From there they looked like tiny overanimated dolls crowding around toy cars and trucks and buses. He turned back to his partner.

"What did the man look like?"

"Thin, wiry, blond hair cut short. About thirty-five. A brown tweed suit not too well cut." Allen sucked on his pipe, trying to keep it going. "I wondered if he might be a cop or a private detective. That's why I asked if you were in any trouble."

"Did he leave his card?"

"No, and he isn't listed under private investigators in the phone book. Maybe he works out of New Jersey."

Neil returned to his chair and stared down at a cost estimate sheet from the Ridgefield nursery without seeing it.

"Want to talk about it?" Allen asked.

"No. It's just Nancy Gilbert, that girl I told you about. She's revived all those rumors about my trying to kill her cousin."

Allen looked horrified. "Oh, my God, not that again!"

"Yes, only worse this round, because it seems nobody has seen or heard of Elaine for over a year, since August twenty-second."

"You mean she disappeared then?"

"I'd say she left town then, rather than that she disappeared, but nobody saw her leave or knew where she was going."

Allen got off the desk and stood looking down at his young partner, his expression grave. "Do you remember where you were on that date, August twenty-second?"

Neil paused in the middle of lighting a cigarette. "Lord, no. Probably at my old office or the apartment I had then." He got his cigarette lit and clicked his lighter shut. "I might have spent the evening with Nellie at the hospital. She was very ill then. It was just after Elaine and I had split and I wasn't going out or seeing people."

Allen nodded solemnly. "I remember." He paused and

pointed the stem of his pipe at Neil. "If I were you, Neil, I'd try to remember."

Neil's eyes widened and he stared at his partner. "My God, you don't think . . . ?"

"I don't think anything, but forewarned is forearmed." Allen smiled thinly. "Frankly, I wouldn't blame you if you had killed the bitch."

"That's not very funny," Neil said, and picked up the cost sheet, trying to conceal his sudden anger.

He spent a nervous, unproductive morning, called off a luncheon appointment with a business associate and ate alone, going back to the hermitlike existence he had endured after his parting with Elaine. When he got back to the office, Harriet Hart had a message for him.

"Miss Colton called from Andrew Crawford's office. She wants you to call her back."

Neil took the note with the phone number and went into his office, wondering if it was a business or personal call. Vicky Colton was a plump little blonde he had dated a few times. She was about his age and had been Andrew Crawford's secretary for several years.

He dialed the number and a brisk voice said, "Crawford, Gordon, Kingman and Lawrence. Good afternoon."

"Miss Colton, please," Neil said, thinking he would go mad if he had to say all those names a hundred times a day.

Vicky's voice finally came over the line. It was a rather nasal, midwestern voice, which was one of the reasons he had not seen more of her.

"Hi, Vicky," he said. "You wanted me?"

"Mr. Crawford does. He's out to lunch now, but wants you to come into the office at three o'clock, if you can make it."

Oh, God, Neil thought, now Andrew was going to get into the act and question him about Elaine.

"All right," he said, wearily. "I'll be there at three."

The offices of the Crawford firm were in one of the sky-scrapers on Park Avenue, just north of Grand Central Station, which he could see from his penthouse. A receptionist with incredible platinum hair and flawless make-up told him Mr. Crawford was expecting him and to go right in, please.

Andrew's office was lavish, complete with thick carpeting, leather sofas and chairs, a bar concealed behind mahogany paneling and shelves of expensively bound legal books. It was at the end of a hall. Bob Ewing's office was halfway down the hall, and Vicky's, between it and her boss's. As Neil started to pass Bob's office, he glanced at his watch, noticed that he had a few minutes to spare and decided to drop in on his friend.

Bob had several books open on his desk and was making notes on a sheet of yellow paper. The wall behind him was solid glass, facing another office building across the avenue.

"Why, hello there," he said, throwing down his pencil and grinning. "What brings you?"

"Andrew wants to see me. Do you know what it's about?"

"No, but it could be about that Morningside Drive property. I know he's had an offer for it and thinks you should sell."

"I was afraid it might be about Elaine."

Bob raised his eyebrows. "Elaine?"

Neil nodded. "You were right about Nancy Gilbert. She's as busy as a hornet stirring up trouble."

Neil told him about his last meeting with Nancy and about the man who had questioned Allen Rutland the day before.

Bob adjusted his glasses and looked glum. "Do you think she's put a private eye to work on you?"

"What else can I think?" Neil's voice was bitter. "She pretends to believe in me when she's with me, but it's obvious now that she thinks something has happened to Elaine and that I . . ."

"Knock it off, Neil!" Bob cut in. "Elaine will turn up one of these days and make fools of all these goddamned gossips. Just keep yourself together until she does." He smiled encouragingly. "Don't let the vultures get to you."

The door suddenly opened and Vicky's blond head appeared.

"Ah, there you are," she said. "The great man is waiting."

Bob grinned. "See you later, and remember what I said."

As they went down the hall to Andrew Crawford's office, Neil asked Vicky if she knew what the meeting was about.

"The Morningside Drive property," Vicky said, then smiled up at him. "How have you been? I haven't seen you for ages."

She was not pretty, but there was something appealing about her. She reminded him of a friendly, round little pony, sturdy and eager to please. He had taken her to dinner a few times and spent several evenings at her little garden apartment on East Thirty-sixth Street, where she lived alone with a poodle named André. He was sure she must have heard about Elaine's accusations against him, but had only heard her mention Elaine's name once.

She had invited him to dinner about a month after his grandmother's death and while they were having coffee afterwards, she had asked him if he had really been in love with Elaine. He had admitted it without elaboration.

Vicky had shaken her head. "That's a damned shame," she said with midwestern candor. "I've never thought she was worth the powder to blow her to hell."

They had never discussed Elaine again.

When they reached the door to Andrew's office, she paused and looked up at him expectantly.

"We must have dinner together sometime soon," he said, getting the message.

Vicky dimpled. "That would be swell." She opened the door and announced him, then left quickly.

Andrew got up from his desk and came forward, waving a cigar in one hand and holding the other out to Neil.

"Good to see you, my boy," he said.

"You too, sir."

They shook hands and Andrew led him back to the big mahogany desk and indicated a leather chair beside it, then returned to his seat, put on his reading glasses and picked up a legal-looking document.

"We've had a very good offer for the Morningside Drive property and I think it's a good time to sell," he said.

He went on to describe the amount of the offer and the terms. Neil listened carefully and agreed that it was a wise time to sell. While the lawyer went into the details, it occurred to Neil that Andrew must have been quite a good-looking man in his youth and probably still had some attraction for women. He was a little overweight, but his perfectly cut suit concealed the flaws and, like his daughter, Kate, he managed a suntan most of the year. Success oozed from every pore of his body, but he was never smug or arrogant. Perhaps that was why Nellie had trusted him to look after her estate when she was gone.

"Well, my boy, how does it suit you?" Andrew asked, taking off his glasses and beaming at Neil.

"Fine, sir."

"For God's sake, stop calling me sir. I'm not *that* old."

Neil laughed, almost weak with relief because it seemed now that Andrew was not going to bring up the subject of Elaine, but to be on the safe side, Neil said he had to get back to his office immediately for an important appointment.

Andrew escorted him to the door. "Going to Kate's this afternoon?" he asked. "She's having a little cocktail party for Oliver's sister who just got into town, you know."

"No, I hadn't heard about it."

The lawyer twinkled at him. "Come anyway. Vicky will be there." A paternal expression came over his face as he opened the door. "You could do worse, my boy. She's a fine girl."

"I know she is and I'd like to go, but I have another date, thanks," Neil said, and rushed off before Andrew could pursue the matter further.

Mrs. Mallory served him a porterhouse steak that night and when he protested that it was big enough for three men, she began to sound like Nellie.

"You hardly touched your breakfast yesterday or today. I don't know what's wrong, sir, but you're not looking well and . . ."

The phone rang, saving him from the rest of the lecture. Mrs. Mallory went to answer it on the kitchen extension and quickly returned.

"It's Miss Colton, sir."

Neil hurried to the den, wondering what Vicky could be calling about. It was seven o'clock and he had seen her only a few hours before.

He picked up the phone and said, "Yes, Vicky?"

"Neil, I have to see you. It's terribly important. Can you meet me at my apartment in half an hour?"

"I could, but I've just started dinner."

"Well, hurry with it. You can still make it by seven-thirty. I wouldn't bother you, but it really is awfully important." She lowered her voice. "I can't say any more now."

He returned to the dining room, and rammed down the rest of his dinner, which brought further comments from Mrs. Mallory. He left her muttering about the state of his health.

Vicky's apartment was on the ground floor of a converted

brownstone on East Thirty-sixth between Park and Lexington. There were a few steps leading up to a small foyer, where the names of the tenants were in brass slits under the mailboxes and each had its own bell. It was exactly seven-thirty when he pressed Vicky's button, then waited for the click that would unlock the inner door. Nothing happened. He pressed again and still nothing happened. He frowned. If Vicky had called from the Vails', which seemed likely, and it was so important, she would have left right away and be here by now. All she had to do was get a cab and drive down Park from Sixty-first Street, not such a long trip.

There were two apartments on each floor of the building, one facing the street and the other, the rear. Vicky had the ground floor rear and the walled garden that went with it. Neil tried the bell again and waited; then he began to feel that something was wrong. It took him a minute or two to figure out what it was. He had only been to the apartment a few times, but each time he had, Vicky's poodle had started to bark the minute he rang the bell, barking loud enough to be heard clearly in the foyer. Now he heard nothing.

He went outside, looked up and down the quiet street and stood there for a few minutes. There was no sign of Vicky. He went back through the glass doors to the small foyer, getting more impatient and worried each second. Finally he rang a bell at random, noticing that it belonged to someone named J. E. Brown. There was a click and he jumped to open the door.

Seconds later, a masculine voice from an upper floor called down, "Who's there?"

But Neil ran down the narrow hall without answering and rapped loudly on the door to Vicky's apartment. He heard nothing at first, then his heart began to pound as he heard not the usual excited yapping, but a whimper from behind the locked door. He knocked again and the whimper grew louder and then there was another sound, a feeble scratching.

"It's all right, André," he called, and then ran back to the foyer, held the inner door open and rang J. E. Brown's bell again.

This time there was no answering click, but heavy footsteps on the stairs and presently a strapping middle-aged man in shirt sleeves appeared on the lower flight.

"What in hell's the big idea?" he asked, glaring at Neil.

"I think there's something wrong in Miss Colton's apartment," Neil said. "Do you know where I can find the super?"

"In the basement of the next building," Brown said, gesturing toward Lexington. "His name's Purdy. If you want to get in again, try someone else. I'm trying to watch the news."

As Neil started down the front steps of the brownstone, he suddenly stopped in his tracks. The bright day was turning into twilight, but it was light enough for him to see a man standing on the other side of the street, a thin, wiry man with short blond hair, wearing a brown suit and a hat perched on the back of his head. Some cars and a taxi or two passed between them, but he could still see the man standing there watching him.

So now he was being tailed, he thought furiously, but there was no time to lose. He hurried to the next building, where there were some steps going up to the entrance and another short flight going down to the basement. He ran down the steps, couldn't find a bell and began pounding on the door.

A thin old man finally opened the door and looked at him over the rim of his glasses. "Place on fire?" he asked.

"No, but I think there's something wrong at Miss Colton's apartment next door."

Mr. Purdy might have been old, but he was quick and spry.

"Just a minute," he said, and sprang back into the apartment, then reappeared with a large ring of keys.

When they reached Vicky's door, the whimpers were louder and the scratching more insistent. Mr. Purdy selected a key, unlocked the door and flung it open, then said, "Oh, my God!"

Neil stood appalled. Whenever he had visited the apartment before, Vicky had been there to open the door for him, smiling up at him, welcoming him warmly while the big apricot poodle, an intelligent, strong dog, greeted him with silent dignity, showing his pleasure with a wagging pompom tail and shining eyes. The living room with its gay colors and soft lighting had always been immaculate. There had been bottles and glasses and an ice bucket on the coffee table and pleasant music from Vicky's FM set.

Now the poodle was crouched in front of them, whimpering as though his heart were broken. Beyond him the room was a shambles, the coffee table and some chairs were overturned, lamps on the floor and a chintz-covered sofa was shoved out of place. Vicky lay in the middle of the room on the white shag rug, crumpled up near the overturned coffee table, her bulging eyes gazing blindly at the ceiling, her face contorted and discolored. Neil knew before he reached her that she was dead.

Mr. Purdy collapsed onto the sofa, staring at Vicky and began to mop his face with his handkerchief. Fighting nausea, Neil kneeled down and put his hand under her breast, knowing it was futile. Her gay cocktail dress seemed hideously incongruous. André crept over and began to lick his dead mistress' face and Neil dragged him away.

"Call the police, will you, Mr. Purdy," he said, "I think the phone is in the bedroom."

"She's been strangled, ain't she? I seen a case like it up in the Bronx."

"It looks like it."

The old man trudged off to the bedroom, still mopping his face. Neil turned away from Vicky and tried to comfort André, and as he stroked the dog, he realized that there was a large swelling on the side of his head, and when he explored the rib cage, André yelped. Neil couldn't do anything for Vicky, so he kept stroking the terrified dog. It seemed obvious that in trying to defend his mistress, he had been savagely kicked.

"It's all right, boy. We'll get you fixed up," he said.

When Mr. Purdy emerged from the bedroom, Neil carried the dog in and shut the door. When he returned to the living room, the super had found a bottle of bourbon and two glasses. He handed a good-sized shot to Neil and then gulped down the other.

"I'll be gettin' back to my place, sir. The police will know where to find me if they want me," he said, and started for the door.

"Don't you think you should wait?"

The old man shook his head. "If I stick around, I'll puke."

Neil went to the bedroom, found the phone and dialed the Vails' apartment. The poodle put a paw on his lap, begging for something he couldn't give.

When the maid answered the phone, he asked for Kate, thinking she could break the dreadful news to Andrew better than he could, but it seemed that the party was over and had been for some time. It had broken up at around seven, the maid said, because there was another party, a buffet, being given for Mr. Vail's sister by some other friends.

Neil found Vicky's address book on the bedside table by the phone and looked up Andrew Crawford's Greenwich number. The housekeeper told him that Mr. Crawford was staying in the city for the night. There was a Murray Hill number listed, too, and Neil suddenly remembered Vicky telling him that Andrew had a small apartment in town, where he kept a spare wardrobe and spent the night after late meetings or parties. The number didn't answer. Bob Ewing's number didn't either. He was probably with Carol, but Neil couldn't remember her last name.

Two uniformed cops from a squad car arrived first, then a man in a business suit, who said he was Inspector Peter Storm of Homicide, and a sergeant named Romano. The inspector was a medium-sized man in his late thirties and carried himself as though he had spent some time in the Army. He had steel gray eyes, brown hair frosted with silver, and rather sharp features, saved from sternness by good-humored lines around his mouth and eyes.

Sergeant Romano was a pudgy young Italian with liquid brown eyes and very white teeth who looked as though he might burst into an aria at any moment. It was apparently his job to take notes while Inspector Storm asked questions.

The next hour was a nightmare. A medical examiner arrived, followed by police photographers, fingerprint men and a man who moved around the crowded room measuring things. Reporters started banging on the door and one of the uniformed cops held them off. One enterprising newsman managed to get into Vicky's walled garden and through the french doors before he was thrown out.

Inspector Storm finally took Neil into the bedroom and the sergeant followed along. Vicky had twin beds. The police sat on one and Neil on the other. André lay on a couch where Neil had put him earlier, panting, his eyes getting glassy.

"You said Miss Colton called you at seven and asked you to meet her here at seven-thirty?" Storm asked for the fifth time. "She called you from the apartment of one Oliver Vail. Is that correct?"

Neil nodded.

"But she didn't tell you why she wanted to see you?"

"No, she just said it was important."

Storm raised a skeptical eyebrow. "And you dropped everything and rushed down here?"

"I wish I had, but I finished my dinner first and got here at seven-thirty, the time she set."

"And then?"

Neil went over the whole thing again, while Romano wrote in his notebook.

"Why don't you ask that guy, Brown, if you don't believe me?" Neil asked finally, his patience wearing thin.

"You could have been in the apartment, strangled the woman and gone out to the foyer again, then rung Brown's bell."

"That's ridiculous. Why would I do that?"

"To get yourself a witness. You say you waited in the foyer when Miss Colton failed to answer your ring, then you went out into the street and waited there a few minutes, looking up and down to see if she were coming. Then you returned to the foyer, rang her bell again and after waiting some more time, you became worried because the dog didn't bark."

"Yes. That's when I rang Brown's bell the first time."

Storm eyed him steadily. "How did you get here, Mr. Stratton?"

"By taxi. I got here at exactly seven-thirty."

"And what time did you ring Mr. Brown's bell the first time?"

"I don't know exactly. Maybe five or ten minutes later. I went out into the street, as I told you, hoping I would see her coming, then I went back to the foyer."

"We have only your word for that," Storm said, rubbing the side of his nose.

A picture flashed into Neil's mind. A picture of a wiry, blond man in a brown tweed suit standing on the north side of the street watching him. He started to tell the inspector that he thought he had been tailed by a man named Sam

Turner and that the man had been standing across the street watching him. Turner must have seen him go out into the street. The front doors were partially glass and the detective, if that's what he was, must have also seen him standing in the foyer, waiting.

Neil's mouth clamped shut as he realized he couldn't tell the inspector about Turner without dragging in Elaine and Nancy Gilbert and exposing the sordid past to the public as well as the police.

"Well, somebody might have noticed me," he said.

"Let's hope so." Storm got up. "I must warn you not to leave town without advising my office first, Mr. Stratton."

"Then I can go now?"

"Yes, but keep yourself available."

Neil got up too, and looked over at André. "Is it all right if I take the dog with me? Whoever did this kicked him in the head and ribs. We can't just leave him here."

For the first time, the inspector's expression softened.

"All right, you can take him." He paused, frowning. "There's a gang of reporters outside. You'll have trouble getting through with an injured dog." He turned to the sergeant. "Have Mac and Gonzales clear the way, Ben."

Neil wound up carrying André through the shouting, pushing reporters. Flashlights popped in his face and the newsmen fired inane questions at him. In the end, he rode home with Mac and Gonzales in their squad car and astounded Ned, the doorman, when he stepped out of it with the big apricot poodle in his arms.

Two taxis pulled up behind the squad car and a bevy of reporters spilled out as Neil rushed into the lobby.

"Don't let any of them in, Ned," he called over his shoulder, and the doorman jumped to close the glass doors behind him.

Mrs. Mallory, having spent years in the households of the

very rich, was rarely surprised by anything. She accepted André calmly, but tears welled in her eyes when Neil told her what had happened. Vicky had been to a couple of parties at the penthouse and the housekeeper remembered her.

"Take the poor thing to my room, sir, and I'll call Dr. Jayson. He's the one who took care of Mike when he had that kidney infection."

"Won't Mike mind a dog in your room?"

"The Van Pelts had three poodles," Mrs. Mallory said with pride. "Mike grew up with them."

Having deposited André on a sofa in the housekeeper's room, Neil went to the den and tried Andrew's Murray Hill number again. There was still no answer. He tried Bob Ewing with the same result. He hung up, thanking God that he had been forced to get an unlisted number because of the publicity after Nellie's death. The reporters would probably get it eventually, but for the moment the line was free.

His nerves still badly shaken, he poured himself a brandy and went back to the phone. The terrible picture of Vicky's face kept haunting him and he kept feeling that he should do something, but didn't know what. He had not been able to help the police much. He had not known the next of kin or exactly where in Ohio she had come from, or much about her private life. Finally, he set out to track down Kate Vail and located her through her maid.

Kate was horrified when she heard the news.

"Do you know where your father is?" Neil asked when she had calmed down.

"I think he was dining at the Coopers'. I'll try to reach him there." There was a pause; then Kate said, "Why on earth would anyone want to kill Vicky. She's . . . was the sweetest girl in the world."

"I don't know, Kate. Do you happen to know where Bob Ewing is?"

"He was at our place earlier. I had a cocktail party for Oliver's sister, but he left when everybody else did. I don't know where he was going. Probably had a date with that blonde he's so cagey about. I wonder why he's so cagey."

"They're waiting for her divorce to go through."

"Well, I'll hang up now and call the . . ."

"Just a minute, Kate," Neil cut in. "Vicky called me a few minutes before seven and said she had to see me. She must have phoned from your apartment. Do you know anything about it?"

"Why, no, but there are phones all over the place and people use them all the time without asking."

"Who else was at your party?"

"Your friend Nancy Gilbert, and Paul Kendell. He's at loose ends while his wife is in Europe. Dad, of course, and some friends of Odessa's."

"Odessa?"

"Oliver's older sister. Terrible name, isn't it? Bobo Babson brought some man I hadn't met before, but I didn't catch his name. Why are you so interested?"

"I saw Vicky at your father's office this afternoon and she didn't seem to have anything on her mind, but when she called me, she sounded very upset. I figured something must have happened between the time I saw her this afternoon and the time she called me . . . maybe something at your party."

"What could have happened, Neil? It was just like any other party, people buzzing around talking to each other and drinking like mad. Vicky always circulates . . . circulated and made people feel at home. That's why I had her to so many of our parties." Kate sighed. "I suppose it was some thief Vicky surprised in her apartment. These junkies . . ."

"The police don't think robbery was the motive. The place was a mess because Vicky apparently put up a fight, but it hadn't been ransacked and her purse with a good deal of money in it was in plain view."

"That's utterly ridiculous. If she caught him before he had a chance to rob her, he certainly wouldn't stick around after he had killed her." Kate sighed again. "Well, I'll see if I can get hold of Dad. He's going to have a fit, poor dear. I'll break it as gently as I can and have him call you."

"Tell him I'm at home."

Dr. Jayson came and examined André, found three broken ribs, the head badly bruised and no skull damage. He wrapped the ribs with tight Ace bandage, gave a pain-killing injection and left a supply of tranquilizers.

"Keep him quiet for the next few days," the vet said. "He's had a rough time. If he won't eat, we may have to try force-feeding."

Mrs. Mallory, hovering over André, looked up and smiled.

"Don't worry, Doctor. We'll take good care of him."

Neil went back to the den to await Andrew Crawford's call.

He didn't hear the house phone ring, but a few minutes later Mrs. Mallory came in to say that Mr. Ewing was on his way up.

"I knew you would want to see him," she said.

Neil nodded. "I'm expecting a call from Mr. Crawford, but he may come without phoning. Will you call down and tell Ned to be on the lookout for him? There's a mob of reporters and he might have trouble getting through."

"Vultures," Mrs. Mallory said, recalling her early days with Neil, when he had still been news and the press wouldn't leave him alone.

Bob arrived a few minutes later, looking pale and tense. Neil had gone to the living room to wait for him and had put out a bottle of cognac and some glasses.

"I just heard about Vicky," Bob said. "Carol and I were in a taxi and the driver had the radio on. They said you had found her body. Is that true?"

"Yes."

Bob flung himself into a wing chair, pushed his glasses up and rubbed his eyes with his fingertips. It was the first time Neil had ever seen him really shaken, but he knew that Bob and Vicky had gone to work for the Crawford firm at about the same time and had been good friends.

"It was a hell of a shock getting it out of the blue like that. I jumped out of the cab and sent Carol on home in it." Bob's eyes lit on the brandy. "Mind if I have a shot?"

"Help yourself."

Bob did, then settled back in his chair. "It must have been hell for you. How did you happen to find her?"

"She phoned me from the Vails' and asked me to meet her at her apartment."

"Do you know why?"

Before Neil could answer, Mrs. Mallory ushered Andrew Crawford in, then discreetly withdrew. Both of the younger men got up and Neil went to greet him, noticing as he crossed the room that the news of Vicky's death must have affected him deeply. His face was gray under his tan and he looked years older than he had that afternoon. Neil settled him on the sofa and poured him a large brandy.

Andrew gulped part of it and looked up at Neil, his eyes sad and angry. "Who could have done such a thing to Vicky?" he asked. "She never hurt anybody in her life."

"I wish to God I knew."

"Some goddamned rapist, no doubt. This city's going to hell. The whole damned country is. Nobody's safe any more."

Neil sat at the other end of the sofa, allowing Andrew time to pull himself together. The lawyer reached into his pocket, brought out a gold cigar case, selected one and lit it, then turned to Neil.

"Before we discuss Vicky, there's something I should tell you, Neil." He hesitated as though embarrassed, then went on. "Elaine's father called me late this afternoon at my apartment."

"Yes?" Neil said, trying to seem calm.

Andrew studied the burning end of his cigar. "He told me that he has known for several days that Elaine was pregnant when she ducked out of sight last year."

Bob gasped, but Neil didn't move.

"Did you know it?" Andrew asked.

"Of course I knew it," Neil snapped. "That's what really broke us up. Nellie was very sick then and I was worried about money and I asked Elaine if she would have an abortion. She refused, claiming that it was too late and against her principles. Then she invented that story about my trying to kill her."

Andrew was looking at him intently now, his expression grave.

"How many people know about it?"

"I never told anybody about it until Nancy Gilbert wormed it out of me. I thought I was speaking in confidence, but she must have told Elaine's father." Neil's eyes were as hard as sapphires. "That's the only way he could have known."

There was a dead silence; then Bob Ewing addressed his boss.

"If you'll excuse me, sir. What did he expect you to do about it?"

"He said he had been thinking it over, but hadn't done anything for fear of annoying Elaine if she is all right, but the more he thought about it, the more he worried about her. He's afraid something has happened to her and he wanted me to get the best private detectives I could find and make an intensive search for her."

"Did Vicky know about it?" Neil asked.

Andrew nodded. "I got her aside at Kate's party and told her the whole thing. Frankly, I didn't want to get involved with it, but I always valued Vicky's opinion and I thought she might have some idea of how to handle it without embarrassment to anybody."

Neil reached for the bottle and poured more cognac into all three glasses, then settled back again. "Did she come up with anything?"

"No, she just looked shocked, which surprised me, because she was certainly no prude, but she did say she thought I should stall Parker off if I could until we could check further."

"Do you think that's why she wanted to see me?" Neil asked. "Could she have thought I didn't know Elaine was pregnant?"

The old lawyer smiled wryly. "I thought you might not have known, but Vicky said I was crazy, that you couldn't have lived with a woman all that time without knowing, and she was right, as usual." His voice choked up and he reached for his brandy, took a sip and looked at Neil. "What about the dog? Didn't he try to defend her?"

The question didn't surprise Neil. Vicky had told him about the Christmas morning nearly three years before when a messenger had arrived with a poodle puppy done up in a large bow, a present from her boss, who worried about her living alone in a garden apartment and had chosen a standard-bred instead of a mini poodle for better protection in case of trouble. She had named him after Andrew and loved him dearly.

"He must have done his best," Neil said. "He's in Mrs. Mallory's room with three broken ribs and a head injury."

Andrew, who loved animals almost as much as he did

people, swore and puffed away on his cigar to cover his emotions.

Bob looked across at Neil. "Maybe it was Parker and not Nancy who sent that man you told me about this afternoon."

"I was just wondering about that," Neil said, then turned to Andrew. "Do you think it's possible that George Parker jumped the gun and hired a detective to check up on me before he called you?"

Andrew shook his head. "He said he hadn't done anything until he decided to call me. Why?"

"There was a man who said his name was Sam Turner in my office yesterday," Neil said, and went on to tell them what his partner had told him. "Allen said that he was about thirty or thirty-five, thin with short blond hair. From his description, I think the same man was outside Vicky's apartment this evening."

"That's strange." The lawyer's tanned face puckered in thought. "We'll have to look into it. Did the police seem to have any idea who killed Vicky?"

Neil told him everything that had happened and about Inspector Storm's lengthy questioning.

"I'm not at all sure they don't suspect me," he added. "Storm suggested that I could have got into Vicky's apartment earlier, strangled her, then gone out again and rung Brown's bell so I'd have a witness to the time of my arrival."

"Oh, for God's sake, Neil," Bob said, "they always grab at straws when they're stumped. Nobody in their right mind would think you killed Vicky."

"It might not be a bad idea to find this man, Sam Turner, anyway," Andrew said. "Just in case."

Bob glanced at his boss. "Sir, what do you intend to do about George Parker?"

A shrewd look came over Andrew's face. "I'll have to head him off somehow. Vicky's death is bad enough without his raising a stink about Elaine just now."

"You might be able to stop Parker," Neil said, "but I don't think you can do anything with Nancy Gilbert. Paul Kendell seems to have convinced her that Elaine left town under strange circumstances."

"What in hell does Kendell know about it?" Andrew asked irritably.

Neil told them about the thousand dollars Elaine had borrowed from the photographer and failed to return. When he had finished, both lawyers looked worried.

"Do you think it would be a good idea for me to tell the inspector the whole thing, about Elaine, I mean?" he asked.

"Good God, no!" Andrew cried.

He got up and strode over to the french doors. Usually the lights on the terrace were lit and made a pretty picture, but tonight nobody had turned them on and Andrew looked at the darkness. When he turned and came back, he was frowning deeply.

"I think we should try to keep Elaine out of this at any cost," he said, sitting down and picking up his cigar. "I don't see how she could possibly be connected with Vicky's death, but if the press got hold of . . ."

Neil interrupted him. "Don't you think it's quite a coincidence that Vicky phoned me just after learning Elaine was pregnant?"

"No, I don't," Andrew said curtly. "She didn't call to break the news to you. We know that because she was sure you must have known. I told you that."

"Then why do you think she wanted to see me?"

"How in hell would I know?" Andrew snapped.

Neil dropped the subject, realizing that the older man was getting tired and the murder of his secretary hadn't done his nerves any good. The picture of Vicky's poor, strangled body flashed into his mind again and he shuddered.

"What will they do with Vicky's body?" he asked.

Andrew looked surprised, as though he hadn't thought of

that point yet. "Well, I imagine they'll release it after they do the usual autopsy and her family will claim it. I believe she only has a widowed mother. Is that right, Bob?"

Bob nodded. "I met her a couple of years ago when she came East to visit Vicky. I took them to the theater. Nice old girl, plain and plump. Worked in some department store, I think. Do you think we should notify her?"

"The police will have done that," Andrew said, "but you could call her and tell her not to worry about funeral expenses or anything like that. Arrange for the shipment of her body, and find out if there is anything else we can do."

"Yes, sir."

"And, Bob, see what she wants done with the dog."

Bob looked puzzled.

"Well, he's her property now," Andrew said testily, "unless Vicky made other arrangements in her will, which I doubt."

"If she doesn't want him, I'd be glad to keep him," Neil said. "Will you tell Mrs. Colton that when you call her, Bob?"

The young lawyer smiled. "Your housekeeper's going to love that."

"She likes animals." Neil reached for the brandy bottle. "Anyone like another shot?"

Andrew shook his head. "I have to be going. Kate wanted me to drop by after I left here." He got up and offered Neil a small smile. "Sorry I snapped at you, my boy. This has been such a shock."

Bob got up, too. "I'll go along with you, sir, in case the reporters give you any trouble."

Neil saw them to the foyer and rang for the elevator. While they waited Andrew laid plans.

"I'll call George when I get back to my apartment," he said, "and I'll tell him he might alienate his daughter forever if she finds out he's been trying to butt into her affairs."

The elevator came and the operator opened the door, but Andrew wasn't finished.

He looked at Neil with another faint smile. "Try not to worry. If things get tough and that man Turner was a detective tailing you, we've got it made. There is a man named Bill Crow who has done excellent work for us. He'll find Turner if anybody can. I'll have him call on your partner in the morning and get a full description."

Neil nodded and turned to the operator. "Are the reporters still downstairs, Jack?"

Jack grinned. "Some of them got sore and left when Ned wouldn't let them into the lobby, but there are still a few outside."

"I can take care of them," Bob said, then put an affectionate hand on Neil's shoulder. "If you want me for anything, just holler."

Neil watched the elevator doors close behind his friends, then breathed a sigh of relief. He was glad they had come and now he was glad they had gone. He had other fish to fry.

❧❦

His other fish was Nancy Gilbert and a few minutes later, he slipped out the service entrance, found a taxi and was headed down Fifth Avenue, getting angrier by the minute. It wasn't bad enough that she had pumped him dry, passed on information he had given her in confidence, and broken promises to him. Now she had the gall to hire a detective to check up on him.

He was in the lobby of her apartment-hotel before it occurred to him that she might not be home, or if she was, might not want to see him, but she was home and told the desk clerk to send him up.

By the time Nancy opened the door for him, he had

worked himself into a fine rage, but she disarmed him by smiling up at him with wet eyes.

"I heard about Vicky on the radio earlier," she said. "It must have been awful for you finding her like that. I tried to phone you, but they wouldn't give me your number."

She ushered him into the drab living room which she had tried to brighten with flowers and some paintings she had brought back from Europe.

"I just made a pot of coffee. Sit down and I'll bring you some."

She trotted off to the kitchen, leaving him deflated. He sat down on the dun-colored sofa, wondering how she could be so devious, pretending to be glad to see him while hiring a man to spy on him. She was back in a few minutes with a tray and chattered while she poured the coffee. Watching her, he was forced to admit that she looked lovely in a pale blue cocktail dress with her light brown hair freshly done.

"I'd never met Vicky until this afternoon at Kate's," she said, "but she seemed like a wonderful person. Cream? How much sugar? Did you know her well?"

He lit a cigarette and crossed his long legs, relaxing a little, despite his mood. "Not very. I had a few dates with her, but that's not what I came to see you about."

Nancy sat down and cocked her head sideways. "Oh?"

He put the cup she had just handed him on the table and looked straight at her. "Why in hell did you put a private detective on me, Nancy?"

Her eyes widened. "Why did I *what?*"

"Oh, come off it. It had to be you or your Uncle George, but Andrew Crawford talked to him this afternoon and he said he hadn't done anything since he learned Elaine was pregnant." Neil's expression hardened. "And that's another thing. When I told you about that, I was speaking in confidence."

Nancy had the grace to blush. "I'm sorry, but I thought he

should know. After all, he might be a grandfather and I didn't dream he would tell anyone else."

"I suppose I should have expected it of you," he said wearily. "You've done nothing but cause trouble for me, but I never thought you'd have the nerve to hire some jerk to check up on me. Where did you dig up Sam Turner?"

"But I didn't, Neil. I swear I didn't. I never heard of the man." Nancy seemed really upset. "Why would I do such a thing?"

He continued to regard her coldly. "The last time I saw you I said the matter of hiring a detective to find Elaine was closed and you said you wouldn't be too sure of it. Do you think I can lead you to her?"

Nancy looked at him pityingly. "I meant Uncle George, you idiot. When I thought it over, I began to wonder if he would really give up so easily. I think now that he told me to drop it because he didn't think I could be impartial about it, or wanted more time to consider what to do."

"Well, he considered it all right. He mulled it over and then called Andrew this afternoon and asked him to start an intensive search for Elaine."

"Is Andrew going to?"

Neil shook his head. "He's calling your uncle tonight and advising him not to start anything just now. We're in enough trouble with Vicky's murder."

"I don't get it." Nancy brushed her bangs aside and frowned. "What's Elaine got to do with Vicky's death?"

"Probably nothing, but it seems odd that Vicky called me just after Andrew told her about Elaine being pregnant. Of course it could have been for some other reason completely. You were there. Did you notice anything unusual? Did Vicky seem upset or anything?"

Nancy looked thoughtful. "Kate introduced me to her when I first got there and I chatted with her for a few minutes. I thought she was awfully nice. Then . . . well, you know how these parties are. I got stuck with a hat designer and then some bores from Chicago. The party was for Oliver's sister and there were a lot of her old friends there, mostly older people. I didn't even see Vicky leave, but it must have been around seven, because that's when the party ended."

"I wondered about that," Neil said. "Those parties usually go on forever. How did Kate get rid of everybody by seven?"

Nancy smiled. "I wouldn't have had the nerve to do it, but Kate can get away with anything. She simply got up and announced that the guest of honor was going on to a buffet given by other old friends and she had to leave at seven, so her party would end then."

"And they all cleared out?" Neil was astonished. "No straggling drunks? It must have been a miracle."

Nancy smiled again. "Odessa's a lot older than Oliver and her friends were all in their fifties and acting like Shriners at a wild convention. Loud and drinking their heads off. I think Kate was afraid they would stick around and freeload for the rest of the evening. Anyway, she simply told them that Oliver would take his sister to the buffet and she would join them as soon as she could get away." Her smile turned into a light laugh. "Meaning as soon as they would get the hell out, of course. It worked and she did it so graciously that nobody seemed to mind."

"Did you go to the party with Paul Kendell?" Neil asked.

"No, I met him there." Nancy looked wistful. "I hoped he'd ask me to have dinner with him, but he had to go back to the studio to finish up some work, so I had dinner at a little place on Eighth Street. I hate eating alone."

She picked up her cup and took a sip of her coffee, then frowned again. "Neil, if Uncle George didn't hire that detective and I didn't, who did?"

"I don't know, but someone did. He was in my office yesterday pumping my partner about me, and this evening

I spotted him outside Vicky's apartment. If it was the same man, he must have tailed me there, in which case I should thank whoever hired him."

"What on earth do you mean?"

"He could verify everything I told the police about when I got there and what I did before I found Vicky's body."

Nancy lowered her cup and stared at him. "My God, Neil, they don't think you . . . ?"

"I don't know what they think, but if they find out the woman I was engaged to claimed I tried to kill her, then left town suddenly and hasn't been heard of since . . ." He shrugged. "That's why Andrew is trying to head your uncle off."

"I suppose he's right," Nancy said, but she looked doubtful.

"Well, his firm is one of the best and most respected in the city and he *is* my attorney. I'd be crazy not to take his advice."

"Did you talk it over with your other lawyer, the young one?"

"Bob Ewing? Yes. They were both at my apartment to-night and they agreed it was the best course to take." Neil's expression suddenly changed. It had been solemn, now it broke out with a smile. "I have a houseguest. He has big brown eyes and curly hair."

Nancy smiled, too. "I'm glad it's a he. Anybody I know?"

"He's a poodle." Neil grew serious again as he went on to tell her about the dog's injuries and how he had found him.

Like Andrew, Nancy was as upset about a dog as she would have been about a person. "What a monster! Kicking a dog that was just trying to defend his mistress. I'd like to get my hands on . . ."

The phone interrupted her. She reached for it, listened, then said, "All right. Ask him to come up, please." She hung up and turned to Neil. "It's Paul Kendell."

Neil got up. "I was just about to leave anyway."

"Don't go. I wasn't expecting him."

He decided to stay because Paul had been at the Vails' and Neil was interested in anyone who had been there when Vicky was. He had often seen the photographer at various parties, but neither of them had sought out the other and they had only a casual acquaintance. Neil had known that Paul had worked with Elaine on some high fashion jobs, but the professional side of her life had never interested him. Now it occurred to him that if Paul had been a little in love with Elaine, as Nancy had suggested, it would account for the coolness he had noticed in the man's manner.

Paul Kendell was a tall, thin man in his early thirties. He had light blue eyes, carrot-colored hair, and although he spent his life working for fashion magazines, he dressed with a casualness that was almost sloppy. His suits were expensive and well cut, but rarely seemed pressed or even clean, and his ties were blindingly gaudy. Neil had always thought of him as a cool customer who never seemed to get emotional about anything, but when Nancy let him into her apartment that evening, he seemed excited.

"Have you heard that Vicky Colton is dead?" he asked, looking down at Nancy as she led him in. "Bobo Babson just called me at the studio. Some bastard strangled . . ." He suddenly saw Neil and stopped short, his pale face turning paler. "Oh, hello, Stratton," he said, "I didn't know Nancy had company."

His manner was even colder than it had been on previous occasions. In fact, it was almost hostile. He refused the coffee Nancy offered him, but accepted a drink, then dropped into a chair and regarded Neil with frank distaste.

"I understand you found Vicky's body," he said, and took a sip of his drink.

"Yes."

Paul continued to look at him. "How come you were there?"

Neil's temper started to flare up. "If it's any of your business, I was there because she called me from Kate's and asked me to meet her there. You were at the party. Did you talk to Vicky?"

"What's that got to do . . . ?"

"Vicky was upset when she called me. I wondered if anything unusual happened at the party."

"Well, if it's any of *your* damned business, I talked to her for a minute or two. If she was upset, I didn't notice it, but then I don't know her very well." The photographer lit a cigarette and leaned back in his chair, his face a pale mask.

"You certainly have bad luck with your women, don't you, Stratton?"

Neil started to jump up, but realized that if he did, he would get into a brawl. He managed to keep his voice under control, but his eyes were blazing. "Just what do you mean by that?"

Paul shrugged. "Seems rather strange that one disappears and the next one gets herself strangled."

Nancy, who had been sitting quietly on the sofa, suddenly came to life. She leaned forward and her usually soft voice was high with emotion.

"Paul, are you insinuating that Neil had anything to do with Vicky's death?" she asked.

The photographer met her furious glare blandly. "Let's just say I think there's something damned queer going on. I wasn't too concerned about Elaine at first, but the more I hear, the more I wonder." His cool glance shifted to Neil. "And now Vicky has been strangled and you just happened to turn up . . ."

Nancy turned to Neil. "Tell him about Sam Turner."

Paul's eyebrows shot up. "Sam Who?"

"He's a private detective somebody hired to check on Neil," Nancy said, her angry words rushing together, "and Neil saw him outside Vicky's apartment after he found her body."

"So?" Paul said.

"So he must have followed Neil down there and he would be able to tell the police exactly when Neil went into the apartment."

"Nancy, for Pete's sake, shut up," Neil cut in. "I'm not even sure it was the same man my partner described and it's no business of Paul's anyway."

Nancy's anger died down as fast as it had risen and she smiled sadly. "I'm sorry, darling, but I just couldn't sit here and let him . . ." Her voice trailed off.

The photographer looked from Neil to Nancy and back again.

"So it's like that," he said, then finished his drink and got up. "I wouldn't have come if I'd known you had company, but I thought you should know about Vicky as soon as possible."

Nancy, obviously relieved, got up to see him to the door, then came back, frowning.

"I wonder what he meant by that," she said. "Why should I know about Vicky as soon as possible?"

"Just a friendly warning about what happens to the women in my life," Neil said, suddenly sick and tired of the whole thing.

"Like a nightcap?"

"No, thanks, I'll have one when I get home. It might help me sleep."

When she saw him to the door, she reached up and put her arms around his neck. He obligingly kissed her.

"Try not to worry, darling," she said softly. "Everything will turn out all right."

Neil's handsome face hardened. "Nothing has turned out all right since I met Elaine," he said, and left Nancy looking after him with apprehensive eyes.

❧

When Neil returned to his penthouse, he found a message in Mrs. Mallory's firm hand. Andrew Crawford had phoned, left his Murray Hill number and wanted Neil to call him back.

Andrew answered immediately. "I just wanted to tell you that I talked to George Parker and he agreed not to do anything about Elaine for the time being," he said.

"That's good. Thanks for letting me know."

"And, Neil, I was right about George. He didn't hire anybody to check up on you." There was a pause and Neil could imagine the lawyer's face puckered in thought. "Are you sure the man was a detective."

"No, but my partner thought so and I'm going only on what he told me. The description he gave fits the man who was outside Vicky's watching me."

"Well, I'll get Bill Crow on it in the morning. Night."

"Andrew . . . ?"

"Yes?"

Neil hesitated, then plunged. "Do you think something might have happened to Elaine after all?"

"Why do you ask?"

"I went down to Nancy's after you and Bob left. I thought she might have put that tail on me, but she swears she didn't. Anyway, while I was there that Kendell guy dropped in and made some cracks I didn't like."

"Like what?"

"He didn't come out and say so, but he seemed to be implying that Elaine is dead and I killed her."

Andrew laughed curtly. "You should know by now that nothing ever happens to dames like her. They just wander around causing trouble for everybody else and come out unscathed."

"But still . . ."

"For God's sake, don't *you* start worrying about it. George Parker is bad enough. As I just told him, she's probably living in some commune with a rag around her forehead eating nuts and fruit."

Neil instantly saw the picture and smiled. "And canned sardines," he said.

❧

His smile did not last long. The image of Elaine wandering around a commune eating nuts faded and in its place he saw Vicky's contorted face. He saw it off and on all night as he tried to sleep, and woke up exhausted and discouraged.

He had a lot of work to do in his office, but he knew from past experience that the reporters would be on his neck until the commotion about Vicky died down. Things had been bad enough after Nellie's death, but with a murder to work on, they would be impossible. He decided to stay home and do what work he could in his den.

When Mrs. Mallory served him breakfast, he inquired about André.

The housekeeper smiled. "He ate a little hamburger and I gave him his pill and he's back to sleep on the sofa." Her smile turned to a gay little laugh. "Mike just sits on the arm of the sofa like an owl, staring at him, but André feels too rotten to care."

When he finished breakfast he went into the den and called his office to say he wouldn't be in. Harriet Hart told him that there were reporters in the hall and others keeping the phones hot. Mr. Rutland was on another line talking to the people in North Carolina.

"Want to wait for him?" she asked.

"No, just tell him that a man named Bill Crow will be in to see him about Sam Turner and it's okay to answer questions. My lawyers are sending him."

"Have you seen the morning papers?"

"No, and I don't want to. I had a bellyful of the press last year."

"There's a big spread of you clutching a poodle on the front page of the *News*."

"If things get too tough, just close the office and go home." Harriet laughed. "Don't worry. I'll cope."

He hung up, thanking God for her diplomacy. Probably no woman he knew could have refrained from mentioning Vicky.

⚜

After several false starts, he finally managed to get to work, but had barely gotten going when the phone rang, startling him. He picked it up warily, afraid that the press might have got his number somehow, but it was Kate. Her normally low voice was so cool he barely recognized it. He was also surprised that she was up, because she never got up much before noon.

"An Inspector Storm was here at the crack of dawn," she said. "What on earth did you tell him about us?"

"Why, nothing, except that Vicky had called me from a party at your place."

"Well, it didn't sound like that. It sounded as though he thought someone who was here had something to do with Vicky's murder. He wanted a list of my guests and asked all kinds of questions. Oliver is furious."

"I'm sorry, Kate, but I can't control what the police do."

"You must have said something," Kate said bitterly. "You asked me yourself who had been at the party. Seems strange they should ask the same things."

"I didn't say anything to them about that, but what are you worried about? They can't involve you or Oliver."

"But they can and they tried to."

Neil scratched his head and frowned. "I don't see how they can when Oliver was taking his sister on to another party and you were following as soon as your guests left."

"How did you know that?"

"Nancy told me. Isn't it right?"

"That was the plan, but it didn't work out that way. Oliver left with Odessa, but when he got down to the street, he realized he was tight. The party was on Central Park West, so he decided to put Odessa in a cab and walk across the park to sober up before the next bout."

"And you?"

"I got rid of everybody, then had to change clothes. One of Odessa's fine friends dumped a drink all over my dress, but before I did, I laid down for a while. Those awful people gave me a splitting headache and the Metcalfs' party was a buffet, so it didn't matter if I was late."

"But surely they couldn't think you or Oliver . . ."

Kate laughed harshly. "Can't they now? They put us through the third degree. It was awful. Oliver didn't know exactly when he got to the Metcalfs' and neither did I. Our maids were in the kitchen cleaning up the party mess and didn't see me go out, and the doorman is a moron. He remembered getting me a taxi, but not when, because there was another big party in the building and he was rushed."

"I'm terribly sorry, Kate, but I honestly didn't say one damned thing to the police except that Vicky had called me from your place."

"But why in hell should that make us suspects?"

"I don't know what angle they are working on, but I do know from what the inspector said that they don't think it was breaking or entering, or that she surprised anyone in the apartment."

He could hear Kate gasp on her end of the line; then she said, "Good Lord, Neil, do you mean they think it was someone she knew?"

"I don't know what they think."

Kate gave another harsh laugh, which was so unlike her. "Well, at least you're in the clear. Dad told us about that detective he can produce if they get tough with you. Oh, here's Oliver. He has a horrible hangover to make things worse."

"Make him a Bloody Mary."

"I just made a big fat shaker of them," Kate said, sounding more like herself again. "I'll explain to Oliver that you didn't put the cops on us. Oh, he's coming in now. Bye, dear."

Neil managed to work until noon, when Mrs. Mallory tapped on the den door and came in, nervously smoothing the skirt of her blue morning uniform, her pleasant face anxious.

"They just called from downstairs to say that an Inspector Storm and a sergeant from Homicide are on the way up, sir."

He nodded, then said, "It just occurred to me that today is Thursday. It's your day off."

Mrs. Mallory smiled tenderly. "You wouldn't expect me to run off and leave my patient, would you, sir?"

Neil smiled, too. "Take the men into the living room. I'll be along in a minute. And thanks for sticking around."

There was no reason he couldn't have let them in himself, but their call had taken him by surprise and he wanted a little time to get ready for another round of questioning. He lit a cigarette and sat smoking it for a few minutes, then squared his shoulders and went to the living room.

Inspector Storm was standing by the hearth, his hands in his pockets. He was wearing the same gray suit he had worn the evening before and looked as though he hadn't had much sleep, but Sergeant Romano's plump Italian face was cheerful and unlined as he turned from the terrace, where he had been admiring the colorful gardens.

"That sure is somethin'," he said. "And right in the middle of New York."

The inspector said he had a few more questions if Neil didn't mind, then crossed to the sofa facing the hearth and sat down, looking at Neil with a faint smile. "You're the fellow who inherited all that money last year, aren't you? I thought I recognized the name. Your grandmother must have been a grand old lady."

Neil sat down too, feeling more relaxed. "Yes, she was."

Sergeant Romano wandered back from the terrace, dropped into a chair and took out his notebook, then waited for his boss to begin. The inspector did so immediately.

"Did you notice a man in a brown suit standing across the street from Miss Colton's apartment last evening?" he asked.

The question startled Neil, but he tried not to show it.

"Yes. I saw him when I ran out to get the superintendent. How did you know about him?"

Storm might have looked tired, but his steel gray eyes were bright and alert. "We questioned everybody in the neighborhood, naturally. There is a Mrs. Zoltan who lives in the second floor front of the building. There have been process servers after her, so she takes a good look before she goes out. She wanted to go to the delicatessen last evening, so she looked out to check first. She saw you arrive in a cab and then, a few minutes later, she noticed this man standing watching the building from across the street. She decided not to go out."

"How long did he stay?" Neil asked.

"The Zoltan woman says he stayed there until the police cars and the ambulance left, then he joined the group of reporters and left with them later." The inspector waited for Romano to catch up with his rapid words, then shot a keen look at Neil. "Had you ever seen the man before, Mr. Stratton?"

Neil realized that it would be to his own advantage to tell the truth, and now that he knew Nancy had not hired the man, he need not bring her into it.

"No, I had never seen him before, but I think his name is Sam Turner and that he is a private detective," he said, and went on to explain why he thought so.

Inspector Storm seemed puzzled. "And you have no idea who hired him or why?"

"No, not the faintest."

"Why didn't you tell me about this when I questioned you last evening?" Storm asked. "If this man was there from the time you got there until you left, he could verify your account of your actions. He could be an important witness for you." He paused, then smiled grimly. "If the story you told me is correct, that is."

Neil lit a cigarette, trying to gain time, then said, "As I just told you, I had only my partner's description to go on, and I wasn't sure it was the same man, and I had no way of knowing exactly when he got there. But I told my lawyers about him and they are trying to find him."

The inspector nodded. "We have a fairly good description of him from Mrs. Zoltan, and Purdy, the super, noticed him too." He turned to the sergeant. "Check it out with Headquarters, Ben. Is there a phone handy, Mr. Stratton?"

Neil indicated the den across the room. "In there, on my desk."

Romano jumped up and headed for the den, his steps light and bouncy.

"Our receptionist tried to find Turner after he left the office," Neil said, "but he wasn't listed under private investigators."

Storm frowned. "If he's licensed to work anywhere in or around New York, we'll find him."

They sat there in silence for a while, then Neil asked if there were any new developments in the case. If there were, the inspector didn't divulge them.

Neil tried again. "Kate Vail called me a little while ago and was upset because you wanted a list of the guests at her cocktail party."

"Not the entire list, thank God." Storm rubbed his lined forehead with his fingertips. "Just the people who knew Miss Colton. That let out most of the guests."

"You're still against the thief theory?"

The inspector's eyes hardened. "It had to be someone she let into her apartment herself and young women living alone in New York these days don't do that recklessly."

"Not unless they're crazy," Neil agreed.

"It seems obvious that she pressed her buzzer to unlock the foyer door and then opened her own door, because she was expecting someone." Storm looked straight at Neil. "She was expecting you, and must have assumed that you had arrived early."

Neil met the detective's hard eyes. "Then you think it was someone who knew I was going to meet her there?"

"It would certainly appear so."

Neil glanced away, cursing himself once more for having finished his dinner while he might have saved Vicky's life if he had left right away.

"You're absolutely sure you don't know why she wanted to see you?" Storm asked suddenly, as though he hadn't asked it repeatedly the evening before.

"Absolutely. I've been asking around to see if anything happened at the party that might have frightened her or upset her, but nobody I've talked to seems to have noticed anything unusual."

The inspector nodded. "We've been doing our own checking." He leaned back comfortably, took a pack of cigarettes from his pocket and lit one, then watched the smoke spiral up.

"I understand you were engaged to a woman named Elaine Parker," he said, almost casually.

Neil's heart started to pound. "Yes," he managed to say, "but it didn't last long and we broke it off over a year ago."

Storm stopped watching the smoke and turned to him. "And nobody has heard from her or seen her for over a year, since August twenty-second. Is that correct?"

"As far as I know," Neil said warily. "I suppose Paul Kendell supplied that information."

"Several people did." The inspector frowned and drew on his cigarette. "Seems strange nobody notified Missing Persons."

"She's often gone away for long periods of time without letting anyone know where she is. Didn't Kendell tell you that?"

"He did, and he also told me that Miss Parker told all her friends you had tried to kill her before she disappeared."

Neil felt his face flush. "Yes, she did. I've never known why, but it might have been because she was angry with me for breaking our engagement."

Storm looked astonished. "You broke it?" he asked.

"Yes," Neil said. "I didn't know then that I'd ever have much money and I was afraid of Elaine's extravagance, particularly just then when my grandmother was very ill and I thought I would be responsible for her medical bills."

"I see." Storm smoked thoughtfully, then turned to Neil again. "Didn't you ever worry about Miss Parker? Wonder what happened to her?"

"No, our break was final." Neil paused, then frowned. "I

really don't see what this has to do with Vicky's death. It's an entirely different matter."

"Did the two women know each other?"

"Yes, but not very well."

The inspector started to say something, but just then Sergeant Romano bounced in from the den.

"There is no Samuel Turner licensed as a private investigator in any of the five boroughs or New Jersey," he said. "They're checking further and will get back to us later. While I was waiting I tried all the Samuel Turners in the Manhattan phone book. There were three. One was a plumber, another a retired jeweler and the third died last June."

The inspector nodded, snubbed out his cigarette and got up.

"Well, we're about through here."

Neil got up and went with them to the foyer to ring for the elevator. It came after what seemed an eternity and then just as the doors opened, the inspector said, "How's the dog?"

"Coming along. The vet's keeping him under sedation for a few days and my housekeeper is taking good care of him."

Unexpectedly, Inspector Storm grinned. "You're a lucky stiff to have that terrace. I have to walk mine every damned night."

The minute he was alone, Neil went back to the den and dialed Andrew Crawford's office. The operator went through her usual routine, then rang Andrew's phone.

"Miss Hilton speaking," a strange voice said.

"This is Neil Stratton. Is Mr. Crawford there?"

"No, Mr. Stratton, he just left for a luncheon appointment. I'm Madge Hilton, his new secretary. Can I help you?"

How quickly a human being could be replaced, Neil thought, then asked for Bob Ewing.

"Hi, Neil. How's it going?" Bob said.

"Not good. I wanted to talk to Andrew, but he's gone out to lunch. Bob, the police were here. They just left. I wanted to tell Andrew we can't keep Elaine out of it any longer. They know all about her."

"Christ, not that she was . . . ?"

"No, but everything else. Paul Kendell and probably Bobo Babson must have blabbed everything. Kendell swears that Elaine disappeared on August twenty-second, and Inspector Storm even knew that."

"You sound worried. Did they give you a hard time?"

"I think Storm is suspicious about Elaine's going off the way she did. He seems to think it queer that I hadn't worried about her or that nobody notified Missing Persons."

"What's he investigating, for God's sake? Elaine, or Vicky's murder?"

"That's not all," Neil said. "There seems to be something odd about Sam Turner. There's no such person licensed as a private detective in New York."

"I thought from what you said that he was a fake, anyway. No competent investigator would be as crude as he was."

"Did you talk to Vicky's mother?"

"No, but I talked to the woman she lives with, a Mrs. Peterson. Seems Mrs. Colton went into shock when she heard the news and had a mild heart attack. She's in the hospital and Mrs. Peterson is taking care of things. She will be here tomorrow to take Vicky's body back and make the necessary arrangements about the apartment and Vicky's stuff."

"Will you tell her that if Mrs. Colton wants the dog, he won't be able to travel for at least a week. He's still under sedation and will be for several days."

"Don't worry. I'll take care of it. Anything else?"

"Yes. Tell Andrew the police are looking for Sam Turner, so he might as well call off his man Crow."

Bob didn't speak for a moment; then he said, "Neil, you sound as though you're holding something back. Want to talk?"

"No, I'm just worried about the whole bloody mess. I thought I was rid of Elaine, but she keeps coming back like some goddamn ghost."

"My God, you don't think the police are going to rake all that up again, do you?"

"They've already started. Have you been questioned yet?"

"Not yet, but Kate warned me they would. Thank God, I went straight from her place to pick up Carol at a hen party, then we had dinner and I was taking her home when we heard the news in the taxi." Bob paused and added, "Want to meet me for lunch someplace and have a few drinks?"

"No, but thanks anyway. I have some work I can do here and Mrs. Mallory is probably already fixing lunch."

"Well, so long then."

Before he had lunch, Neil went into Mrs. Mallory's room to see André. The dog was lying quietly on the sofa, his bandages in place around his ribs. The side of his head was not so swollen and he wagged his tail feebly when Neil spoke to him. The Persian, his new-penny eyes wide, was perched on the arm of the sofa, his expression alert and watchful.

Mrs. Mallory came in and patted André's curly head. "He'll be needing a clip when he's better," she said fondly.

André rolled his eyes at her in a sad imitation of the gay way he had flirted with Vicky. Neil gathered him up in his arms and carried him to the terrace for his airing. Mike followed, his plumed tail in the air. Neil set the big poodle down and watched with mounting anger as André tottered around on the grass. He could have strangled whoever had done this to a brave dog trying to protect his owner. On the trip back to the sofa, André lifted his head and gently licked Neil's cheek, thanking him.

"Maybe Miss Colton's mother won't want him," Mrs. Mallory said brightly as she served lunch. "He's such a wonderful dog."

Neil smiled. "I hope not, but we can't get too attached to him until we know."

Their eyes met and both of them knew that it was already too late. Even the cat had fallen for André.

The afternoon went as calmly as it could under the circumstances. Neil worked in the den, André slept on the sofa and Mike dozed on the sunny terrace, taking a break from his vigil; then Mrs. Mallory went out to do some shopping and brought the evening paper back with her. She took it to the kitchen to read before she started dinner, as she usually did, but after glancing over the front page, she hurried into the den with it, put it down on Neil's desk and pointed.

Neil looked down and gasped. Elaine's beautiful face was on the lower part of the first page, the dark eyes staring at him, the small, sexy smile taunting him. Above the photograph was the headline: MODEL REPORTED MISSING— and under it, the story of how Elaine Parker, a beautiful model, had disappeared on August 22 of the previous year and was being sought by the police, who feared foul play. Anyone having information as to her whereabouts or any other information was to get in touch with the police at once.

The story went on, describing Elaine and mentioning that she had last been seen by fashion photographer Paul Kendell, on the day of her disappearance. There was no mention of the money she had borrowed from him, but the story did say that she had been staying at the Drake Hotel after closing her beach house in Westport, Connecticut.

Neil finished reading the article, thanking God that there was no mention of him, then looked up at Mrs. Mallory, who was standing by the desk. He had no idea how much she knew of his relationship with Elaine, which had been before her time with him, but her anxious expression told him that she had heard enough to worry.

"Well, let's hope they find her," he said, keeping his tone light.

Mrs. Mallory picked up an overflowing ashtray. "She's Miss Gilbert's cousin, isn't she, sir?"

He nodded, not even bothering to ask her how she knew. From his youthful experiences with his grandmother, he knew that servants knew everything. Mrs. Mallory left with the ashtray and Neil glanced at the paper again, idly noticing that there had been another fatal mugging in Central Park. An unemployed newspaper reporter named Irving Walsh had been robbed and stabbed.

The report went on to say that Walsh, thirty-four, of 138 West Sixteenth Street had apparently been stabbed at about midnight the night before, but his body had not been discovered until late that morning, when some children playing had found it behind a clump of bushes near the East Sixty-fifth Street entrance to the Park.

Mrs. Mallory returned with the clean ashtray, put it down and after telling him he was smoking too much, glanced at the paper again. "Poor man," she said, shaking her head. "Unemployed and they rob and kill him. Probably got a dollar or two. What's the world coming to?" She went out, still shaking her head.

The phone rang just as she closed the door. It was Nancy, sounding breathless. "I got your number from Kate," she said. "Have you seen the evening paper?"

"Yes."

"Well, I wanted to let you know that I didn't report Elaine missing and neither did Uncle George. I just called him. The police . . . that Inspector Storm and his sergeant were here this afternoon, but I was very careful about what I said."

"What did they question you about?"

"You. I would have called you sooner, but I couldn't reach Kate to get your number until a few minutes ago."

"What did they want to know about me?"

"If you seemed normal to me." Nancy still sounded breathless. "If you were subject to sudden rages. Did you drink much? Stuff like that; then they asked me if you had ever discussed Elaine with me and I said, naturally, since I was her cousin and you had been engaged to her, but I didn't go into any details." She paused for breath, then said, "I didn't like that bit about sudden rages, Neil. What do you think they were driving at?"

Neil frowned and lit a cigarette, his handsome face flushed.

"I don't think we should discuss this on the phone, Nancy. Would you like to come up for a drink and stay for dinner?"

"I'd love to, darling. I'll change and be right up."

He had just hung up when Mrs. Mallory came in with the news that Sergeant Romano was on the way up.

Christ, what now? He got up wearily and downed a neat scotch before the sergeant bounced into the living room, his dark eyes shining.

"Inspector Storm sent me to ask you if you would mind meeting him at the City Mortuary, sir."

Neil stared at him. "Do you mean the morgue?"

"Yes, sir. Would you come along with me, sir?"

"Who's dead?"

"A newspaper fella, a reporter named Irving Walsh." Romano's round face looked like a child's with a surprise. "We think he might be your friend, Sam Turner."

Neil turned pale, then excused himself to go and tell Mrs. Mallory Nancy was coming for dinner and that he had to go out for a while; then he returned to the living room, where the sergeant was admiring the gardens again.

"Sure is beautiful," he said smiling. "My father was a gardener."

Neil smiled back. "I am, too; a landscape architect."

"No kidding?"

Neil had never been in a morgue before or anywhere near Bellevue Hospital and he found the whole thing depressing, as he followed the cheerful sergeant through a maze of corridors, finally ending up in an antiseptic-looking room where Inspector Storm was talking to a man in a white uniform.

"Sorry to trouble you again, Mr. Stratton," the inspector said, "but we think we have located the man you described. Your partner, Mr. Rutland, is inside now."

In sharp contrast to his sergeant, Inspector Storm looked worried, and the lines on his face were even deeper than they had been that morning. He introduced the man in white, but Neil didn't catch the name. Probably someone in charge of records, because there were files around the room and a ledger on the desk.

A few minutes later, Allen Rutland came through a white door with a glass inset at the top. He was accompanied by another man in white, who looked like an aging albino bloodhound. Allen had a handkerchief over his mouth and looked on the verge of throwing up, but when he saw Neil, he pulled himself together, removed the handkerchief and tried to smile.

"It's the same guy," he said. "God, the smell in there."

Inspector Storm stepped forward. "Would you mind, Mr. Stratton?" he asked, indicating the bloodhound with his head.

Allen looked at his partner ruefully. "Sorry I can't stick around and wait for you, Neil, but it's Samantha's birthday and I'm terribly late for the party as it is. It's her twelfth birthday."

"That's all right," Neil said. "I'm sorry about all this."

"How could you help it?" Allen asked, and hurried out.

It wasn't long before Neil returned to the room, feeling as rocky as his partner had looked. The drooping attendant had pulled out a drawer and he had gazed down at a white, freckled, dead face. It was not the face of a strong man, but in death there was a touching innocence about it.

"Well?" Inspector Storm asked.

"I can't be sure, but he looks very much like the man outside the apartment. Was he wearing a brown tweed suit?"

The inspector nodded. "And a brown felt hat." He sighed deeply. "I guess that wraps it up. Come on, Ben. Work to do."

Neil followed the two policemen through the corridors until they came out into the late afternoon sunshine. They crossed the crowded sidewalk to the waiting police car. The sergeant went around to the driver's side and Inspector Storm looked at Neil.

"Where were you at midnight last night?" he asked flatly.

"I went down to see Nancy Gilbert and left about eleven-thirty. It took me a while to find a cab and I got home a few minutes before midnight, I think. But I'm not absolutely sure."

"Perhaps Miss Gilbert will remember when you left."

"If you're looking for her, she is probably at my apartment. She's having dinner with me."

"A charming girl." A thin smile toyed with Storm's mouth, but his eyes were like steel and his hair seemed more frosted with silver in the sunlight. "Seems strange to me that she hasn't been more concerned with her cousin's disappearance."

"They haven't seen each other in years," Neil said, instantly on the defensive.

The inspector turned and started to get into the car, but Neil said, "Inspector . . . ?"

Storm looked over his shoulder. "Yes?"

"Why did you put that Missing Persons bulletin on Elaine Parker?"

"Because if she's alive I want to talk to her and if she's dead, I want to know it," Storm said grimly, and got into the car.

When Neil got back to the penthouse, he found Nancy in Mrs. Mallory's room. She was sitting on the floor beside the sofa, feeding André bits of ground round, and he was taking them politely. She was wearing a beige silk cocktail dress that matched her light brown hair and she smiled as he joined her.

"Why didn't you tell me he was so adorable?" she said. "He's probably heartbroken, but trying so hard to be dignified about it."

She took a closer look at Neil and her smile faded.

"Are you all right? You look awful. What's the matter?"

"I've just been to the morgue. They found Sam Turner."

Nancy fed André the last of the meat and put the new dog bowl on a table. They went into the living room together and this time Nancy made the drinks while he collapsed on the sofa facing the hearth, leaning back with his eyes closed, his face white. Nancy didn't say anything until she had made the drinks and put them on the cocktail table. His was a stiff scotch, hers a martini. When she curled up beside him, he opened his eyes and put his arm around her.

"Did you read about the reporter who got mugged and stabbed in Central Park last night?" he asked.

Nancy frowned lightly. "Yes. It was just next to the thing about Elaine, but his name wasn't Sam Turner."

"No, it was Irving Walsh and he was the man I saw outside Vicky's." Neil took a long pull on his drink. "My partner identified him as the man who was in the office asking about me."

"My God, Neil," Nancy said, her eyes wide with horror. "He could have confirmed your story of what happened at Vicky's and now he's dead. It wasn't just another mugging, was it?"

"I suppose it could have been, but it doesn't seem likely." Neil looked puzzled. "I can't figure out what an unemployed reporter was doing following me and questioning people about me *before* Vicky's murder. I haven't been news for a long time."

"The paper said he had a wife and two kids and had been on welfare since his unemployment insurance ran out. He must have been having a rough time."

"I know, but why me? What did he expect to get from me?"

He glanced at Nancy as though she could answer him, but she could only shake her head hopelessly. They sat there silently for a few minutes, lost in gloom; then Nancy brightened.

"At least they can't think you had anything to do with Turner's . . . I mean Walsh's death," she said. "That's the only good thing about it."

"I'm afraid not."

"Why not? You'd hardly kill a man who could back up your account of when you got to Vicky's and what happened."

"Or make a liar out of me if I hadn't been telling the truth."

Nancy looked startled. "What do you mean?"

"Nobody but Walsh could have seen me waiting in the foyer. It has glass doors and he would have been able to see me, and he would have known I went out and stood for a while looking to see if Vicky was coming."

"That's what I meant," Nancy said.

"And it's the truth, but without Walsh, I can't prove it. As far as the police know, I could have gotten into the apartment right away, strangled Vicky and come out again to raise an alarm. They could assume that if I had been lying Walsh could have proved it and I could have killed him to prevent his talking."

Nancy reached for his hand, held it tightly and looked at him with tears in her eyes. "Neil, I'm scared. There's somebody loose killing people and each time it seems to involve you."

He picked up his drink with his free hand and drained it, his expression strained and tense. "I've sworn I never wanted to see Elaine again, but now I hope they find her and force the truth out of her."

"The truth?" Nancy said, looking blank.

"About that night on the beach when she said I tried to kill her." Neil released his hand, got up and went to mix himself another drink. When he returned, he sat in the wing chair near the sofa as though he did not want to be too close to Nancy.

"I've got to know the truth about that, Nancy," he said, his blue eyes piercingly bright. "Either one of us was nuts and having hallucinations, or one of us lied. And I didn't lie."

Nancy brushed back the hair at her temple and regarded him curiously. "I thought you had put that out of your mind months ago. You said you had."

"Nobody had been killed then. It seemed just a matter between Elaine and me and I knew I hadn't lied about it, but now it all seems to go back to that night. It's as though there is something strange and evil going on, but I didn't realize it until Vicky's death." Neil scowled at his drink. "And now this poor devil Walsh. It seems I'm somehow responsible for his death too."

Nancy leaned forward, her face suddenly pink with emotion.

"Stop talking like that, Neil. You went to Vicky's because she asked you to, and it certainly wasn't your fault that Walsh man was snooping around and following you."

"That's just it," Neil said. "I'm in the middle of something and I don't know what. I don't know why Vicky wanted to see me or why Walsh was dogging me. I'm up against something I can't see." His scowl deepened. "If the police don't believe me, they'll be after me too. It's as though some invisible net is closing in on me and I can't do anything about it."

"For heaven's sake, don't get paranoid about it," Nancy said with a forced smile.

"*Paranoid?*" Neil's voice rose. "Is that what you think? That I'm paranoid?"

"Oh, cut it out." Nancy continued to smile, but her eyes were anxious. "You sound like a second-rate Irish playwright."

"Thanks."

Mrs. Mallory saved them from an argument by coming in to announce dinner.

While Nancy and Neil were pretending to enjoy Mrs. Mallory's superb cooking, Inspector Storm and Sergeant Romano were in a Howard Johnson's outside Stamford having hamburgers and coffee. They were on their way to Westport to interview a woman who had phoned in to say that in late August of the previous year, her thirteen-year-old son had found a suitcase washed up on the beach.

"Of course, it could be anybody's suitcase," the inspector said, but there was a light in his eyes.

"Yeah," Romano said, munching his second hamburger.

Inspector Storm looked thoughtful. "Any one of them could have knocked off Walsh. Neil Stratton says that he left

Miss Gilbert's hotel at about eleven-thirty, walked for a while before he found a cab, and got home just before midnight, but the spot where Walsh was found is only a minute or two away from his apartment. Give me the rundown on Andrew Crawford again, Ben."

Sergeant Romano got out his notebook, put it on the table and began flipping the pages. "At the time of the Colton woman's death or Walsh's?"

"Both."

"He claims that after he left his daughter's party, he stopped by his apartment on East Sixty-fourth to pick up a wallet he had forgotten when he went there to change before the party. No confirmation. It's a two-room apartment with a self-service elevator he uses when he's in town late and to change before dinner or cocktail parties. He keeps a spare wardrobe there."

The sergeant winked. "Maybe that's not all he does there. Anyway, he stopped off there for a while, then went on to a dinner party given by some people named Cooper on Park and Sixty-first, but it was a big party and nobody could vouch for the time of his arrival."

"And later?"

"When his daughter located him and told him about his secretary's death, he went to see Neil Stratton, then back to the Vails'. He claims he left there a little after eleven and went to his apartment and turned in."

Inspector Storm finished his coffee and ordered more, then frowned as he lit a cigarette. "It's the same with all these damned so-called socialites. Parties, never sure when they get where. Boozing it up. Take young Ewing. He picked up his girl . . . what was her name?"

Romano consulted his notes again. "Mrs. Carol Laird. She's in the middle of a divorce, trying to get a big settlement, so she's cagey about being seen in public with Ewing. He claims he picked her up at the St. Regis after he left the

Vails' party. She was at some sorority cocktail party. He took her to dinner at a place called Luigi's on Third and was taking her home in a cab when he heard about the Colton woman's death. He went straight to Stratton's apartment, same as Crawford."

The inspector nodded. "Then after he left Stratton's he went to Carol Laird's apartment for a while, then home to his apartment on East Fifty-eighth, near Second Avenue. Again no witnesses. It's a duplex in a remodeled town house. Very swank bachelor job, according to Mahoney's report."

"And the Vails went to bed after Andrew Crawford left." The inspector sighed. "They were sound asleep before midnight and so was the help. It's all so goddamned pat."

Sergeant Romano flipped more pages and smiled wryly. "And Paul Kendell left Miss Gilbert's apartment just before Stratton did and went to his apartment on West Tenth. A walk-up. Want the rundown on the model, Bobo Babson?"

For the first time in hours, Inspector Storm really smiled.

"No, she couldn't strangle a mouse and we know she went to dinner with the man she took to the Vails' party. He spent the night with her. My only interest in her is what she had to say about the Parker-Stratton relationship."

Their fresh coffee came and the inspector waited impatiently while Sergeant Romano ate a serving of peach-pecan ice cream.

"You don't think Walsh's death could have been just another mugging, do you, sir?"

"Hell, no. Again, it's too pat, and what was he doing there at that time of night? He lives down on West Sixteenth Street. Why wasn't he home with his wife?" The inspector took a deep drag on his cigarette and answered himself. "He was there to meet someone and whoever it was killed him and stole his wallet to make it seem like a mugging."

The sergeant nodded agreement and took another scoop of his ice cream.

"He must have been there for a payoff of some kind." Storm signaled for the check and got up. "For God's sake, stop fooling with that mess. We've got things to do."

Mrs. Irene Vance was a gracious brunette in her late thirties with an earnest manner and candid eyes, her face plain, but attractive. Her house was on a road paralleling the beach. She led the detectives into a nicely furnished living room, explaining as she went that her husband was in Chicago on business and that she had sent her son to a neighbor's.

"There's nothing Victor could tell you that I can't," she said, smiling, "and in case this is connected with Elaine Parker's disappearance, I would prefer not involving a child."

"Did you know Miss Parker?" Storm asked.

"None of us knew her, but we certainly knew *of* her." Mrs. Vance indicated a large tan suitcase she had placed on a luggage rack in the middle of the room.

"What makes you think it might belong to Miss Parker?" Storm asked, noticing that there were no initials on the suitcase, only the trademark, Samsonite, on a small brass plaque near the handle.

"The papers said that Elaine Parker disappeared on August twenty-second and Victor found that suitcase the next morning. It hadn't been in the water very long and I thought at the time that it might have fallen from some yacht."

Inspector Storm had opened the suitcase and began to examine its contents, holding up each item, then handing them to Romano.

"There's nothing of any real value except for a gold locket with a diamond in it, but the dresses are expensive and there is a mink hat and muff set that must have cost a lot."

"They look in excellent condition," Storm said, looking over a brocade cocktail dress.

Mrs. Vance smiled again. "When Victor showed up with the case, I opened it, naturally, and when I saw how expensive the clothes were, I was sure someone would be looking for them, so I dried everything out. The case must have been nearly airtight, because some of the things were only damp. I rinsed some out and sent the rest to the cleaner's. When my husband got home he phoned the police."

"Did they take any action?" Storm asked, turning to her.

"No. They just told Jim they would refer any inquiries to us and took the phone number."

Mrs. Vance lit herself a cigarette and looked anxiously at the inspector. "I didn't think of it until I read that bulletin in the paper, but I could swear I've seen Elaine Parker in that red bikini you've got in your hands now."

Storm felt the thrill of the chase, but remained outwardly calm. "What did you mean by saying none of you knew Miss Parker, but knew *of* her?"

"Well, we'd all seen her in *Vogue* and *Harper's*, of course, and knew who she was, but she was never friendly, never spoke to any of us, even a few of the older people who remembered her as a child."

"An anti-social type, you'd say?"

"When she was out here, definitely, but from the gossip columns it was very different when she was in the city." Mrs. Vance grinned wickedly. "We'd see her on the train, looking beautiful and smart, but the rest of the time she would be on that sun deck of her beach house, nearly naked and there was a man, a very handsome young man, who practically lived there with her. Later, he was in all the papers. Inherited a lot of money, but then he didn't seem to have much."

"Then you didn't know him either?"

"No, but Jim, my husband, used to catch the same trains he did on weekends and sometimes during the week. He never spoke to anybody either. Jim says she must have worn him out. He started off all happy and gay, whistling as he walked down the station platform, but that by the end, he began to look tired and harassed."

Mrs. Vance tapped ashes from her cigarette into an ashtray and her grin disappeared. "Needless to say, we were all glad when she closed her house and left, particularly the parents with young daughters."

Sergeant Romano had been spreading the dresses on the sofa across from Mrs. Vance and now it was covered, as though a salesman were displaying his wares. Inspector Storm reached into a side pocket of the suitcase and came up with the gold locket.

"There's nothing inside," Mrs. Vance said. "I looked."

She was right. There was nothing in it and the inspector returned it to the side pocket and instructed Romano to repack it.

The sergeant's dark eyes rolled. "Jeez, Inspector, I dunno . . ."

Mrs. Vance laughed and got up. "I'll do it for you."

While she packed, she rattled on. "I notified the Yacht Club and the Coast Guard, but when nobody showed up to claim it, I decided to take it to the Salvation Army or the Thrift Shop, but I never got around to it." She laughed again. "Maybe I wouldn't have been so charitable, but they're all size fourteen and I'm a ten."

The detectives stood awkwardly by while she carefully folded the dresses and tucked them in. When she had finished she turned to Inspector Storm, her eyes curious.

"Inspector, a friend of mine who lives down that way called me a little while ago and told me there are men digging all around the Parker place. Do you expect to find . . . ?"

"We don't expect anything, Mrs. Vance," Storm cut in. "We are simply trying to locate a missing woman."

"Do you think the suitcase is hers?"

"We'll find out soon," Storm said. "Perhaps her friends can identify the clothes or the locket."

"That young man should know. God knows he must have seen enough of that bikini if nothing else." Mrs. Vance looked prim. "And some of the boys say she didn't always wear that."

The phone rang and she crossed the room to pluck it from a small desk, then held the receiver out. "It's for you, Inspector."

Storm took it from her and heard Lieutenant Nelson's voice from Headquarters. He listened, frowning and making notes on a pad that lay beside the phone; then he thanked Nelson and hung up.

"Do you know a man named Peter Grimes, Mrs. Vance?" he asked.

"Why, yes. I was just talking to his wife before you got here. He owns the Marina."

"That was Headquarters." Storm's glance went to his sergeant. "Grimes phoned in to say that one of his customers' boats turned up missing on the morning of August twenty-third, a fourteen-foot sloop. Grimes said he couldn't understand it at the time because it had been securely tied up at the dock."

"I was just going to tell you about that," Mrs. Vance said brightly. "Harriet Grimes told me about it when I told her about the suitcase."

"How do we get to the Marina?" Sergeant Romano asked, picking up the suitcase.

"We don't," Storm said. "He told Nelson he was home and would wait for us there."

"They live just a few blocks from here," Mrs. Vance said, and proceeded to give them directions.

Storm made out a receipt for the suitcase, which she carefully put in the desk drawer; then she escorted them to the door.

"We may have to ask your son to show us exactly where he found the suitcase, but it can wait until tomorrow," Storm said.

"Oh, dear, must you?" Mrs. Vance turned on her welcome lights, then went out to the sandy lawn with them and pointed into the darkness. "There is an old beach road over there and some summer cottages along the shore. Victor found the suitcase washed up on the beach there. He had gotten up before dawn to surf cast and there wasn't anybody else around."

"Where is the Parker house from here?"

"About a quarter of a mile down the beach on a little inlet."

The inspector thanked her and went to his car, the sergeant tagging along with the suitcase.

Peter Grimes was about sixty, a sturdy man with curly, iron-gray hair, keen blue eyes and a weatherbeaten face. His wife was a plump little woman with white hair and a maternal way. After the detectives had introduced themselves, she insisted on going off to the kitchen to make them coffee.

The house was an old one, carefully preserved and comfortably furnished. Grimes settled his guests, sat down in an overstuffed chair and came right to the point.

"This might have nothing to do with Elaine Parker's disappearance, but I thought it might interest you." He picked a dead cigar out of an ashtray and relit it. "I read about Elaine in the paper, but didn't connect until Irene Vance

called my wife a little while ago and mentioned the suitcase
her son had found."

Sergeant Romano had his notebook on his knee and was
writing furiously. Grimes, noticing it, slowed down.

"We all knew about that strange suitcase," he went on,
"but had forgotten about it; then when Irene mentioned it
to my wife, she suddenly remembered the Butlers' sloop.
When I came home for dinner, she asked me if I knew exactly when the boat had turned up missing. I didn't, but I
phoned the Marina and asked my manager to check. It was
the same morning the Vance kid found the suitcase, August
twenty-third."

"Tell me about it," Storm said, trying again to conceal his
excitement.

"Well, the Butlers planned to take a run up to New London that day and make an early start, so we brought the
sloop in from its mooring the evening before and tied it
up for them. But when they got there it was gone. The
Coast Guard found it that afternoon out in the Sound with
its jib flapping."

"Then whoever took it must have known something about
sailing?" Storm asked.

"Yes." Grimes's sharp eyes met the inspector's. "You're
not looking for Elaine, are you? You're looking for her body.
My manager saw men all over the Parker place when he
sailed by this afternoon. And the paper said you suspected
foul play."

"That's true," Storm admitted.

"I think you're wasting your time digging around on
shore." Grimes took his cigar out of his mouth and studied
it, then waved it in the direction of the Sound. "I'd bet my
last buck she's out there somewhere and you'll never re-
cover the body."

"Why do you say that, sir?"

"Isn't it obvious? Elaine disappears on the twenty-second

and the next morning the sloop is missing and the suitcase is found. Want to know what I think?"

Inspector Storm looked at his host thoughtfully. "Yes, I do. You know these waters and things we don't know."

"Well, the Parker place is on one side of a small point on an inlet. My Marina is about a half a mile to the south in a sort of cove. Between them the beach is shaped like a long crescent moon. My guess is that if someone had stolen the sloop that night, they would have sailed across to the Parker place, tied up at the old dock and loaded from there."

"Is it deep enough?" Storm asked.

Grimes nodded. "At high tide, yes. The sloop draws only a few feet, but it would have been tricky getting out to the Sound from there. It was a fairly rough night with some wind and I'd think the person sailing her would have had to follow a line running not far from the shore before tacking over and beating against the wind to get out to the open water. I remember the wind and the seas because we checked everything when we found the sloop missing."

"What's your guess about the suitcase?"

"That when this person changed course to head out, the sloop probably heeled over sharply and the suitcase fell overboard. The place where it was found is about halfway between the Marina and the Parker dock." Grimes laughed nervously. "Of course, I'm no Perry Mason, but it would explain the suitcase being found where it was and not being waterlogged, and Irene Vance says some of the clothes were only damp."

Inspector Storm seemed puzzled. "If the sloop was found out in the Sound, how do you figure this person got ashore?"

"Easy," Grimes said. "Anyone who knew beans about sailing could have brought her in close enough to swim for shore, lowered the mainsail, set the jib and dived off. If I had been doing it, I'd have brought her in near the point. It must have been pure luck that the sloop didn't pile up.

The winds out there are very tricky and change with the speed of sound."

Mrs. Grimes came in with a tray loaded with cups and plates of cake and a large coffee pot. The sergeant's eyes lit up, but his boss could only think of getting back to the city. He fidgeted while Mrs. Grimes poured the coffee and served the cake.

"Thank you, dear," Grimes said, then looked at Storm solemnly.

"I can add that if Elaine was in the Butlers' sloop, she'd have had to be dead or unconscious when she was taken aboard."

Mrs. Grimes sat down with her coffee and nodded.

Her husband went on. "When she was about fifteen or sixteen, one of the local boys took her out in his outboard. They got caught in one of those sudden squalls the Sound is famous for and the boat capsized. They were in the water all night before they were found. Wild horses couldn't have got her in a boat after that."

"Then you knew Elaine?" Storm asked.

"Oh, yes. I knew her as a child and as a teen-ager, and I knew her parents," Grimes said. "In fact, my father sold George Parker that property years ago. George was a swell guy, but his wife, Betsy, was a little queer. Artsy and vague."

His wife nodded again. "Elaine was a beautiful child, but she was shy and secretive. As a teen-ager, she was impossible. Voluptuous beyond her years and still childish and selfish. Seemed to think she was some kind of genius and off in a dream world half the time. The other half she was teasing the boys and driving her mother crazy. She wouldn't help with housework or any of the chores."

"Did you see her that last summer she was here?"

Grimes answered, looking indignant. "We saw her all right, but that was all. Harriet called and invited her to dinner, but she said she was too busy working on her poetry."

"She practically told me she couldn't be bothered," Mrs. Grimes added. "Actually, she was too busy with that young man, the one who inherited all that money later."

"Did you ever meet him?"

Grimes shook his head. "She had him all wrapped up, the poor devil."

"Why do you say that?"

"Well, I wouldn't like to have my son involved with a woman like her. Let's put it that way," Grimes said.

❧

It was about nine-thirty when Oliver Vail phoned the penthouse. Neil took the call in the den.

"Is Nancy with you, Neil?" Oliver asked.

"Yes. She came up for dinner."

Oliver's voice sounded strained. "Look, I don't know what's up, but Inspector Storm wants you and Nancy to be here at ten o'clock. He asked me to round up you two and Andrew, along with Bobo Babson, Bob Ewing and Paul Kendell. He wants everybody here by ten."

"You don't know why?"

"A meeting of some kind to identify something he thinks might be evidence." Oliver laughed bitterly. "He seems to think one of us is running around murdering people."

Bob Ewing was already at the Vails' when Neil and Nancy arrived and he did not look happy about it. He was hunched over the bar, nursing a tall drink, but he smiled when he saw Neil.

"Carol is getting fed up with my dashing off and leaving her alone all the time," he said, then greeted Nancy.

He had changed his mind about her since learning that Paul Kendell had been responsible for her renewed concern for her cousin and had triggered her probing at Bobo's party.

Oliver was behind the bar with the air of a man determined to make the best of things.

"What'll you have, kiddies?"

Neil took a weak scotch and Nancy didn't want anything.

Kate came in, flashing her white smile and looking majestic in a black dinner dress. The silver wings of her new, short hairdo set off her perpetual tan and if she was upset about the meeting she did not show it.

She greeted her guests as though it were a social occasion, sat on a bar stool and leaned toward her husband. "I'll have a brandy, darling." Then she turned to the others. "Dad's not a damned bit pleased at being dragged in from Greenwich at this time of night. He says that if this Inspector Storm keeps harassing us, he's going to speak to the commissioner."

Oliver grinned at her. "Well, it beats being hauled off to the jaily-house for questioning."

"But what the hell does he want with us?" Bob asked, adjusting his glasses. "He's already questioned all of us."

He was wearing a gay plaid sports jacket and a white turtleneck sweater. Neil noticed with amusement that there was lipstick on the neck of the sweater. Bob had changed in the past few months, since he had met Carol. His hair was longer and he had grown sideburns. His features were a little blunt, but regular and, oddly, his horn-rimmed glasses became him.

Paul Kendell arrived with Bobo Babson. He was wearing the same suit he had worn the night before and a hideous tie, but Bobo was done to the teeth. Her tall, willowy body was encased in a black sheath and her shiny, platinum hair hung down over her shoulders. A cloud of heavy perfume came in with her and her green eyes were bright in her dead white face.

She smiled at her host and hostess, greeted Bob warmly, ignored Nancy and stared briefly at Neil, her eyes cold and hard. Then she turned to Oliver.

"I'll have a crème de menthe, Ollie. Maybe with a brandy floater," she said with a slight lisp she had culled from old Marilyn Monroe movies.

"What about you, Paul?" Oliver asked.

"Nothing, thanks." Paul scratched his kinky red hair and smiled wryly. "I want a clear head for this séance."

Oliver made Bobo's drink and pushed it across the bar. As she picked it up, she spilled some on her dress and said, "Oh, shit."

Andrew came in a few minutes later, wearing one of his expensive gray Italian silk suits and an irritated expression.

"The law not here yet?" he asked, looking at his watch. "It's five minutes after ten. I don't see why this thing, whatever it is, couldn't wait until morning."

He was sleek and polished, as usual, and his bronzed nearly bald head shone. His pale eyes were shrewd and cautious.

Oliver leaned across the bar. "Do you have any idea what this is all about, Andrew?"

"No, but I don't like it." Andrew glanced at the people scattered around the bar. "I don't know what the inspector has on his mind, but I'd like to make it clear that none of you has to answer any questions you don't want to." He turned to Bob. "Is everything settled about Vicky?"

Bob nodded. "Campbell's is taking charge until that friend of her mother's gets here in the morning." His dark eyes glistened. "It's a damned shame they had to do an autopsy on her body."

"Yes," Andrew said, "but it's the law."

Nancy edged her way toward the older lawyer. "Andrew, can I ask you something?"

"Hello, dear." Andrew beamed at her. "You can ask me anything."

"Does the dog have to go too? I mean, well, maybe Vicky's mother can't take proper care of him and . . ."

"That is up to Mrs. Colton, my dear. Vicky's will left everything to her and the dog is part of her estate."

Andrew looked inquiringly at Bob, who shook his head. "We won't know until Mrs. Peterson, the mother's friend, gets here. I still haven't been able to communicate with Mrs. Colton."

A maid came in just then and announced that Inspector Storm had arrived and was on his way up.

As if on signal they all moved away from the bar. The women seating themselves in a cluster of sofas and chairs around a huge cocktail table at the end of the room, the men, with the exception of Paul Kendell, who flung himself down on a sofa next to Bobo, remained standing, or moving around nervously. There was a sudden tension in the air and none of them spoke.

It seemed to take forever for the inspector to ride up from the lobby, but he finally strode in, looking grim and businesslike. Although his dark suit was a little wrinkled, his stiff military bearing was more apparent than ever. Neil looked around for Sergeant Romano and spotted him near the foyer, as though waiting in the wings.

Oliver went to meet Storm, brought him back to the group around the cocktail table and offered him a drink. The inspector refused and sat down on a flame-colored armchair, where he could observe the others who were settling down. Oliver joined his wife and father-in-law on a wide sofa, Kate in the middle. Nancy and Neil huddled together on a fat, flowered love seat across from the inspector and Bobo and Paul Kendell were on a sofa to his right, facing the Vails. Bob Ewing chose a hassock beside Neil and put his drink on the floor.

"What's the meaning of this, Inspector?" Andrew asked, puffing up like an angry pigeon. "I don't like being dragged out at this time of night."

Storm regarded him without emotion, then glanced around at the others, as though appraising each one. He hesitated to gain their full attention, then sprang his bombshell.

"We have reason to believe that Elaine Parker is dead," he said, and his dark eyes darted around, trying to catch each reaction.

Neil Stratton's handsome face turned white and he glanced sideways at Nancy, who reached out and took his hand. Bobo Babson couldn't turn any paler. She simply stared at the inspector, her mouth a little open. Bob Ewing looked startled, then frowned and shook his head, as though he didn't believe it.

Kate and Oliver exchanged worried glances over her father's head, but Andrew didn't notice it. He lit a cigar and looked at Storm over the flame of his lighter, obviously studying the man, trying to assess his ability.

Only Paul Kendell failed to react.

"I've been saying that for a long time, Inspector," he said, raising his chin with a certain arrogance; then his pale blue gaze shifted to Neil. "I'm sure she was murdered not long after she left my studio that day in August and I've said so, but nobody would listen to me."

Andrew glared at him. "Your personal opinions have no place here, Kendell." He turned to Inspector Storm. "I assume you have good reason for making such a statement?"

Storm nodded and beckoned to Sergeant Romano, who had inched toward them, gripping the suitcase firmly. He had evidently spoken to the maid, because she followed him with a luggage rack and placed it in the middle of the room, then left hastily. Sergeant Romano opened the suitcase and stood beside it.

"We have reason to believe that suitcase belonged to Elaine Parker," Storm said, "but we need positive identification of the contents. If you don't mind . . ." He got up and went over to the luggage rack.

The others got up too, and followed him, forming a sort of circle around the open suitcase. Romano reached down, picked up a ruby-colored cocktail dress and held it up.

Neil stared at it and gasped. It was the dress Elaine had worn the first time he had met her here in this very room.

"Oh, my God!" he said, and turned away.

"That's Elaine's," Bobo said. "I was with her when she bought it at Bergdorf's."

"That's why I wanted you here tonight, Miss Babson," Storm said. "You lived with Miss Parker for a while, so I was sure you would recognize her clothes."

Bobo reached down and pulled out the brocade dress. "This is hers too. She bought it after she modeled it in a fashion show at the Waldorf." Her glance went to Neil, her eyes glittering emeralds, but she said nothing more.

Storm reached into the side pocket and brought out the locket.

"That's Elaine's," Nancy said, blinking back tears. "Her mother gave it to her for her sixteenth birthday."

Andrew stood, looking down into the suitcase, his face expressionless; then his attention shifted to Storm.

"Where did you get this, Inspector?"

Storm turned to Sergeant Romano without answering.

"I guess that's enough, Ben," he said, and returned to the cluster of furniture.

The others followed again and took the same places around the cocktail table, except the Vails, who sat beside each other this time, with Andrew on the end of the sofa closest to Inspector Storm.

Romano pulled up a chair and got out his notebook.

"Would you mind answering my question, Inspector?"

Andrew asked impatiently, flourishing his cigar and crossing his plump legs.

"Well, we've had reports of Elaine Parker being seen all over the country, of course. That always happens, but none of them have checked out."

"You said you had reason to believe she was dead," Andrew persisted. "Have you found her body?"

"No." Storm looked bitter. "And we may never find it."

"Then what makes you think she's dead?"

"Sergeant Romano and I spent the evening in Westport," Storm said. "That suitcase was found washed up on the beach between the Marina and Elaine Parker's house on the morning of August twenty-third of last year, the day after her disappearance. On the same morning a sloop was found missing from the Marina. It was apparently stolen during the night."

He went on to tell them of his interviews with Mrs. Vance and Peter Grimes, owner of the Marina. They all watched him like hawks, all but Neil, who was smoking and staring into space. Nancy sat beside him, her tears drying, her hand firmly in his.

When the inspector had finished, Andrew looked dissatisfied.

"That's slim evidence to say the least, Inspector. Wouldn't her body have washed ashore if your theory is correct?"

"It's much more than a theory, Mr. Crawford," Storm said grimly, "and the body would not have surfaced if it was weighed down, which we believe to be the case. The Connecticut State Police have been making a search of the Parker property at our request. They were looking for evidence of a crime in the house, or the body of Elaine Parker buried on the premises. But after what we learned this evening, we concentrated on finding out if anything that might have been used to weigh down an object had been taken away from the place."

Storm's glance shot to Neil. "Do you remember a concrete block barbecue on the south side of the sun deck at the beach house, Mr. Stratton?"

Neil looked startled and color rushed to his pale face. "Why, yes, I do. I put it together, but I didn't cement it, because Elaine wasn't sure she wanted it there permanently. She thought she might like it better down nearer the beach."

A picture of Elaine in her red bikini, lolling on the canvas deck chair while he broiled steaks, flashed through his mind and he swallowed hard. Those had been the happy days.

"Six concrete blocks from one side are missing," Storm said. "Was it intact the last time you saw it?"

"Yes."

Bob looked up at his friend from his hassock and without speaking got up and went to the bar. He returned with a stiff brandy, and handed it to Neil, who took it and gulped part of it.

"Thanks, Bob," he said. "I was feeling a little queer."

"I know. It's a shock, no matter what has gone before."

Bobo Babson suddenly stood up. "Can I go now, Inspector? I left my guests in the middle of a party and they're waiting for me."

"Yes, you may go, Miss Babson," Storm said, astonished by her attitude. Hard as nails, he thought.

Paul Kendell got up, too. "I'll go along with you, Bobo," he said, then looked down at Storm. "I left my date at Bobo's party and I'll have to see her home."

"No, sir," Storm said harshly. "You'll stay right here until I'm through questioning you."

Paul looked surprised, but sat down.

Bobo bid them good night and crossed to the foyer, exhibiting her slinky model's walk.

Inspector Storm leaned back and lit a cigarette, nodded to Romano to indicate that he should start taking notes, then turned to Andrew Crawford.

"I understand that you keep a yacht at your home in Greenwich, sir.",

Andrew shrugged. "I have a Walton H-28 ketch, but I don't know that I'd call it a yacht. I haven't used it much since my wife died, but Kate and Oliver sail her often."

Storm suddenly shifted to Neil. "And you, Mr. Stratton. Do you know anything about sailing?"

Neil flushed again. "Yes, I learned at summer camps when I was a kid, but I haven't been in a boat for years, not since I was at Cornell."

"And you, Mr. Ewing?" Storm asked, looking at Bob. "I believe your family has a summer place in Maine?"

Bob smiled crookedly. "Now, how in hell did you know that? Yes, they have a place at Kennebunkport and I usually spend my vacations there. And I can sail a boat if that's what you're driving at."

The sergeant was making notes furiously when Storm finally turned to Paul Kendell, who answered before the question was asked.

"I've sailed with Oliver and Kate a few times and with other friends now and then, but I don't really know much about it." He spoke with the same arrogance he had displayed earlier, then looked put-upon. "I honestly don't see why you're questioning me. I'm the one who has been insisting that something must have happened to Elaine. Would I do that if I'd had anything to do with it?"

"That's an interesting question," Storm said dryly, then asked them all where they had been on the day of August twenty-second and the following night.

Paul Kendell was the only one who seemed able to remember.

"I had an appointment with Elaine that morning, as you know," he said. "She was late and we worked until about one. She left then, after asking me to lend her a thousand bucks. I've already told you that. I spent the afternoon raising it from friends and was back at my studio by five-thirty, when Elaine came back. She stayed a few minutes, then left. I finished up my work and went home at about six-thirty."

"Did you go out again?"

"I had dinner there, if you could call it that, then went over to Bobo's to see if she would like to take in a movie, but she was out, so I went by myself, then home and to bed." Paul sighed. "I go to a lot of movies when my wife is away on her buying trips."

None of the others could remember where they had been or what they had been doing during the time in question.

"It was a working day for most of you," Storm said. "I would like you to consult your office records and engagement books . . . anything that might help you account for the time."

He pulled out an envelope with some private notes on the back.

"Elaine Parker left the Drake Hotel with her luggage at eight o'clock that morning. We don't know whether she left in a cab or someone was waiting for her outside. She had to go somewhere with her luggage and leave it, because she didn't have it with her when she got to Kendell's studio." Storm glanced at Paul. "That correct?"

"Yes. I tried to find out where she was staying or what her plans were, but she was evasive."

"The Drake is only a few blocks from Grand Central Station," Kate said. "She could have checked her luggage there."

Storm nodded. "She might have."

"Or she might have taken it out to the beach house that morning," Kate went on, as though working on some kind of interesting puzzle.

"For God's sake, darling, use your head," Paul drawled. "How could she have gone to Westport and been at my studio at ten-thirty?"

"Well, then she must have gone there later, if the inspector's theory is right," Kate said defensively. "Her suitcase *was* found out there."

Paul's unemotional eyes lit up. "Never!" he said flatly. "After she was almost killed there, she wouldn't have gone near it for anything on earth. She told me so dozens of times."

Andrew snubbed out his cigar and got up. "I guess you're through with us now, Inspector. If you don't mind, I have to get back to Greenwich tonight. Golf date in the morning."

He started to leave, then turned back to Bob. "When you meet that Mrs. Peterson tomorrow, be sure she understands that I'm meeting all the expenses involved and if Mrs. Colton needs any help, financial or otherwise, we'll be glad to do everything we can."

"Yes, sir," Bob said.

When her father had gone, Kate smiled proudly. "Isn't that just like Dad? Always thinking of other people."

Inspector Storm got up and looked at Nancy, his eyes for once soft. "I'm sorry about your cousin, Miss Gilbert, and I hope you won't mind, but I'll have to keep her effects for the time being. Matter of evidence."

"I understand," Nancy said. "Do you think I should call her father. I know you usually notify the police in the area and have them break the news, but Uncle George is quite ill and I might be able to soften the blow."

Inspector Storm agreed, thanked them all for their cooperation and the Vails for the use of their apartment, then left with Sergeant Romano again lugging the suitcase.

The minute they were gone, Bob Ewing got up and glanced around at the others. "I don't think Elaine is really dead," he said. "It's the flimsiest evidence I've ever heard of. Don't you think so, Oliver?"

"Beats me," Oliver said. "I'm parched. Who'd like a drink?"

"I would, now that the séance is over," Paul said, then looked at Bob with a shrewd gleam in his eye. "You know damned well Elaine is dead, Bob. You're simply denying it because Neil is one of your firm's richest clients and you're his personal attorney. Anything for the buck."

Bob's dark eyes blazed behind his glasses. "You keep your goddamned mouth shut, Kendell. If Elaine is dead, Neil couldn't have had anything to do with it. He couldn't have got near her with a barge pole and you know it."

"Not if she expected it," Paul said.

"You damned bastard." Bob lunged at the photographer, raising his fists.

Oliver's hefty body was suddenly between them, his friendly, slightly battered face stern. "If you guys are going to start a brawl, you'll have to do it somewhere else."

Paul backed down instantly, his thin face turning pink. "Sorry, Oliver. Forget the drink. I have to get back to Bobo's and pick up Ruthie."

Bob waited until Paul was well on his way and then he left too, anxious to get back to Carol.

Oliver looked after him. "He's really got it this time," he said, then turned to Neil and Nancy. "One for the road?"

Nancy shook her head. "No, thanks. I want to get home and call my uncle."

Neil got up and spoke automatically, like a man in the throes of a bad dream. "I'll see you home," he said.

After they had gone, Oliver went to work behind the bar and Kate sat on a stool across from him.

"Do you think Elaine is really dead, Oliver?" she asked.

Oliver dropped some ice into a glass and frowned. "If she is, they're going to have one hell of a time proving it," he said grimly.

Neil and Nancy hardly spoke on the long taxi ride down to her hotel. He kept staring at the picture of their driver under its little light. Nancy tried to get his attention a couple of times, then gave up.

The apartment seemed more somber than ever when they finally got there. The paintings could not overcome the drabness of the furniture and the hothouse flowers had no fragrance to cover a musty smell. Nancy opened a window, then turned to Neil, who had collapsed on the sofa and was rubbing his forehead with his fingers, his eyes shut.

Nancy sat down beside him, but he seemed unaware of her. She looked at him anxiously for some time, then broke the tense silence.

"Something is bothering you, isn't it?" she asked. "Something more than learning Elaine is dead."

Neil lowered his hand and opened his eyes. "I keep wondering about that night she claimed I tried to kill her," he said, staring into space. "I was awfully upset that night. Do you think I could have pulled a blank and tried to kill her without knowing it? She told people I was either a liar or crazy, you know."

Nancy reached out for his hand and gripped it hard. "No, I don't, not for a second."

He turned his troubled eyes to her. "But if Storm is right, someone did kill her only a few days later. I can't think of anyone else who would have any reason to do it."

"My God, Neil, you're not suggesting that you . . . ?" Nancy stared at him, horrified.

"I've heard of cases where people committed crimes without knowing it," he said. "I knew those concrete blocks were there and just where the Marina was. I used to walk over there and look at the boats."

"For God's sake, darling, stop talking like that," she cried. "I suppose you'll be telling me next that you strangled Vicky and stabbed that reporter."

"No, I'm just talking about Elaine. Some thief could have

killed Vicky and Walsh could have been knifed by a mugger, no matter what Storm says."

"Stop it!" Nancy said, almost screaming. "You really will drive yourself mad if you keep this up."

Neil removed his hand from hers and lit a cigarette, trying to get control of himself; then he smiled sadly at Nancy.

"I'd better go home. I'm not fit company for anybody."

Nancy regarded him silently, then cocked her head to one side, and her expression became tender, like that of a mother with a beloved problem child.

"Do you want to spend the night here with me?" she asked.

The question did not seem to surprise Neil or even excite him. He merely gave her another sad, tired smile and shook his head.

"No, darling. I'd like it more than anything in the world, but not under these circumstances. Not after what happened to Elaine."

"The hell with Elaine!" Nancy's eyes flashed angrily. "What's she got to do with us?"

Neil's face suddenly became very pale and he ran his fingers through his hair despondently. "For God's sake, Nancy, can't you understand? Elaine is dead and I might have killed her. I hated her as much as I once loved her. I didn't want her to have my child. I wasn't normal after we split up. I might have done anything."

"But you couldn't hurt anybody, darling," Nancy said, "I just know you couldn't."

Neil shrugged. "That's what they are always saying about a rosy-cheeked schoolboy who has just clubbed his parents to death with a baseball bat."

"Oh, Neil, what am I going to do with you?" Nancy leaned back, as though exhausted, then gathered her forces again. "Do you know where you were the day Elaine disappeared?"

Neil shook his head. "Only vaguely. My partner suggested that I try to find out when I told him what was going on. I was working on a small job at the time, landscaping a private home in Bronxville. I'd thrown my desk calendar away at the end of the year, and didn't keep any records, but I must have been in the office that day because I wrote some business letters."

"Then your secretary . . ."

Neil interrupted her. "I couldn't even afford a public stenographer then and I did all my own correspondence. I couldn't have gone to Bronxville that day, because I wrote the owner and enclosed some new plans and asked him to let me know if he approved."

"Then you can account for some of the day, anyway," Nancy said, looking hopeful. "You were in your office."

"All I know is that I usually worked the whole day on plans when I had a job, unless I was out at the site or buying stock from various nurseries. I don't know how long I was in the office that day."

"What about that night?"

Neil frowned and took a long drag on his cigarette. "I probably had dinner somewhere and then went up to see my grandmother. She was at St. Luke's up on Amsterdam Avenue." His haggard glance swung to Nancy. "They don't keep records of visitors, but Nellie was very ill during that period and I must have gone there if I wasn't . . ." His voice trailed off.

"Where did you live then?" Nancy asked quickly.

"I had a one-room apartment on West Seventy-second, near Riverside Drive, one of those old mansions they cut up into small apartments." Neil's frown deepened. "I have no way of knowing whether I spent the night there or not."

Nancy's patience suddenly gave way. "What in hell are you trying to do, Neil? If you're trying to convince me that you killed Elaine, you can clear out right now. You're just torturing yourself and I've had a bellyful of it."

Neil colored and his eyes were too bright. "How do you know I didn't kill Elaine?" he asked.

Nancy burst into tears and threw herself into his arms. "Don't talk like that, darling. Please don't."

He gently pushed her away and held her shoulders, forcing her to look at him. "Nancy, I love you," he said, "and I'd ask you to marry me if it weren't for this mess, but I loved Elaine too, in a different way, and look what happened. She's dead and I might have killed her."

He gathered her close again and stroked her silky hair. "I can't risk you, darling, not until I'm sure about myself."

"I'm sure of you," Nancy said. Her cheek was nestled against his chest and her voice muffled.

"I'm not, and I won't be until I'm sure I'm sane and didn't have anything to do with the attack on Elaine or her murder."

She drew away from him, her sobs stopping abruptly, her despair turning to anger. "So, Elaine wins again," she said. "She was the one who started that bit and now you've talked yourself into believing it. I'm disgusted with you."

Neil gave her a long, hard look, then ground out his cigarette and got up. "I think I'd better be going," he said.

"I think so too," Nancy smiled bitterly. "I don't like homicidal maniacs hanging around."

He stood looking down at her for several minutes, then turned and went to the door.

❧

Bob Ewing was in his office working on some briefs when he was surprised to get a call from Nancy.

"I have to see you, Bob," she said, sounding very upset.

"It's one now. Could you meet me somewhere for lunch?"

"Something wrong?"

"Yes, it's Neil. I'm terribly worried about him."

"What about the Oak Room at the Plaza?" Bob asked, instantly thinking of his favorite spot. "I can meet you there at one-thirty, if that suits you."

"I'll be there."

Bob hung up, then took off his glasses and rubbed his face with both hands. He had spent the night with Carol and a miserable morning with Mrs. Peterson, who had flown in from Ohio on an early plane, and he was exhausted. The one good part of the morning was that it was over. He had met Mrs. Peterson at the airport, taken her to Vicky's apartment, arranged for the shipment of her things and returned to the airport to see the woman off. Campbell's had seen to the rest, thank God.

He got to the Oak Room early and was working on his second martini by the time Nancy joined him, looking trim and pretty in her little black suit, but he saw the anxiety in her eyes the minute the waiter seated her across from him. He had gotten up to greet her, then sat down again.

The waiter hovered.

"I think I'll have a martini, too," Nancy said, smiling up at him. "Very dry."

Bob offered her a cigarette and lit it for her, then pocketed his lighter. "What seems to be the trouble?"

Nancy studied him for a moment, noticing for the first time that he was a very attractive man. The glasses didn't spoil his good features or make him look bookish. His dark hair was perfectly cut, and his sideburns, which were as long as Andrew would permit, gave him a dashing look. His shoulders were broad and almost inviting under his well-tailored sports jacket.

"I know you're Neil's best friend as well as his lawyer, or I wouldn't have come to you," she said.

Bob smiled encouragingly. "You're right."

Nancy told him about the scene she'd had with Neil the night before.

"He seemed to think he might have tried to drown Elaine and that if he did, he probably killed her later." Nancy looked at him eagerly. "You don't believe that, do you? You don't think he could have . . . ?"

Bob picked up his glass and frowned at it. "I didn't see much of him that summer. The firm sent me to Dallas to handle a long, involved tax case. When I came back, I went up to Maine to spend my vacation with the family. I was there when he and Elaine broke up, but I was back the next week and saw him. He was in very bad shape, on the verge of a breakdown. Then Elaine started those stinking rumors and he withdrew into his shell. Wouldn't do anything for days on end."

Nancy's eyes widened. "Do you mean he was temporarily insane, out of his head?"

"Good God, no. It was just that he'd been madly in love with Elaine and the break really shook him. Then his grandmother was on the way out and that added to the strain. He adored the old girl." Bob took a sip of his drink and put the glass down. "Everything hit the poor guy at once."

Nancy sat smoking quietly, her fine-boned face white; then she looked up at Bob. "Do you know if he ever had any mental problems before he met Elaine?"

Bob seemed surprised, then smiled. "The only troubles he had were financial. I knew him for a year or so before Nellie died, you know. I took over her affairs when old man Harrison retired and it used to kill me seeing him so worried about money when I knew how much he would come into when she went."

"It must have been hard not to tell him."

"It was murder, but if I'd dropped the slightest hint, I'd have been out of a job. Andrew trusted me and I represented the firm, so I had to keep my mouth shut." Bob's dark eyes shone with happy memories. "The only thing I could do was take him around town and catch the tabs. We had a hell of a lot of fun together."

Nancy smiled, pleased to know that there had been a time when Neil had been happy; then the worry came back.

"Bob, Neil knows he was in his office that day Elaine disappeared, but not for how long, and he has no idea where he was that night. He thinks he might have visited his grandmother in the hospital and then gone home, but he isn't at all sure."

"Simmer down," Bob said. "How many people would know where they were on a given date over a year before? In fact, Andrew called me from Greenwich just before you phoned and asked me if I knew where he had been. We were both in the office all that day, but neither of us can account for the evening. I didn't know Carol then and was playing the field."

He paused to finish off his martini and beckon the waiter, then looked at Nancy.

"I'll stick with this, thanks," she said.

Bob ordered, then went on. "I probably had a date with some chick or went to a party. I know I wasn't with Neil, because he was in his shell and wouldn't come out to play."

Nancy perked up. "And Andrew doesn't know where he was that night either?"

"He's sure he must have been in Greenwich, because he checked with his club and their records showed he had played golf the next morning. And he thinks he must have gone somewhere for dinner, because it was a Thursday and the help was off."

"I don't see how anybody would know unless they kept a diary," Nancy said.

"That's just it. Storm has us all nuts. I called Kate hoping to hell I might have seen her that evening, but she couldn't remember. All she knew was that she was in the city. She and Oliver have a cottage in Southampton. She spends her summers there and Oliver goes out on weekends, but that week she had a long, painful session with her dentist. She doesn't keep her engagement books after they're used up, but she called her dentist and found she'd had appointments three days that week and doesn't think she would have gone out to Southampton at all during that time. With extractions and bridgework she was feeling rotten."

"Does Oliver remember anything?"

Bob shook his head. "They only keep one maid on at the apartment during the summer and she was off. He remembers Kate feeling lousy and thinks he might have whipped up some supper. He's a good cook when he wants to bother and she might have felt too bad to go out to dinner."

He stopped short and smiled at Nancy. "So you can tell Neil he's not the only one who . . ."

"But it's not only that," she cut in.

Bob's smile died when he saw how serious she looked. "Then what is it?"

"You know about Elaine, don't you?" Nancy's question was tentative, as though she was uncertain of how much to say.

"That she was pregnant, you mean?" Bob's manner was casual and reassuring. "Yes, I know, but I don't see what that has to do with anything. It could happen to anybody."

Nancy slowly shook her head. "He doesn't see it that way. He thinks he might have killed her because he didn't want her to have the baby and that no one else had any reason to kill her."

"Oh, for Christ's sake," Bob said, suddenly exasperated. "What's he trying to do, talk himself into believing he's a murderer?" He scratched a sideburn and made a wry face. "He probably feels guilty about the kid, but so what? He couldn't have afforded Elaine or the baby, so he took the only way out. He asked her to postpone the wedding and when she refused he asked her to have an abortion and when she wouldn't do either, he broke the engagement. What else could he do?"

Nancy didn't look reassured at all. She looked frightened.

"But what if Inspector Storm finds out she was pregnant?" she asked.

"How can he?"

Bob picked up the new drink the waiter had just put in front of him and then ordered their lunch. Nancy only wanted an omelet, but Bob, having skipped breakfast to meet the early plane, ordered a rare steak, then turned his attention back to Nancy.

"Only Elaine's father and Andrew and you and I know about it," he said. "Besides Neil, of course, and her father is certainly not going to go around bragging about it. I know you can keep your mouth shut and wild horses couldn't get it out of Andrew or me." He took a sip of his martini and looked across at Nancy. "Did you phone her father?"

"Yes."

"How did he take the news?"

"Quite well, as though he had expected it and was glad to have it over. At least that's the way he sounded to me. He's been quite ill and the worry hasn't helped him." Nancy took a cigarette out of Bob's pack and he lit it for her. She noticed then that he looked tired and remembered that Andrew had dumped the arrangements for Vicky in his lap.

"You must have had an awful morning," she said.

He nodded. "The worst I've ever lived through, but Mrs. Peterson, the mother's friend, was a nice woman, very businesslike. She arranged to have all Vicky's stuff shipped out to Ohio. A friend of Vicky's from the office came down to help and it went off smoothly. I had arranged with Campbell's to deliver the coffin before plane time and had to see to the loading."

Bob grabbed his drink and gulped it down, his dark eyes misty.

"I got them off all right, but it was hell thinking of Vicky in that box."

"Did you talk to her about the dog?"

"I told her he wouldn't be able to travel for a few more days and she's to let me know what they want done with him after she talks to Mrs. Colton." Bob looked sympathetic. "Don't get your hopes up, sweetie. Mrs. Peterson said Mrs. Colton is planning to retire and might want him."

Their lunch came and they switched to other subjects until they had finished; then Bob looked at his watch and frowned.

"Well, I'd better be getting back to the office. Andrew has a batch of British investors and their lawyers flying in from London tonight for a big conference in the morning and the place is a madhouse."

"But isn't tomorrow Saturday?"

"Yes, that's why they wanted it then, between the time that the stock market closes today and opens Monday. Some big financial deal, I guess, and they're afraid of a leakage."

"I was hoping you would go up to see Neil with me later. Maybe you could convince him . . ."

"Tell him there's nothing to worry about. He wouldn't have had to kill Elaine to get rid of her, for God's sake. She was leaving town to get away from *him*. As for the police, they can't produce a body, let alone prove a murder."

He signaled to their waiter for the check, then turned back to her. "Are you going to see Neil now?"

"No, I don't think so." Nancy sighed. "I guess I'll go home. He might call."

Bob paid the bill, then looked down at Nancy with a crooked smile. "Just don't let him crawl back into that shell again."

Outside the hotel, he waved for a taxi and as it approached, Nancy turned to him. "Did you mean it last night when you said you didn't think Elaine was really dead?" she asked.

Bob opened the cab door for her. "I don't know what the hell I meant. I was just sore at that bastard Kendell for trying to hang a murder on Neil when we don't even know for sure there was one."

"Well, thanks for lunch, and be sure and let me know about André, won't you?"

"If Mrs. Peterson doesn't call me, I'll give her a ring in the morning." Bob grinned. "If you want me again, give a yell."

✄

Nancy went home and spent the rest of the afternoon trying to read a new book. The apartment hotel had a restaurant downstairs, but it was expensive and she was trying to economize until she could get a job, so she put a frozen chicken pie in the oven, mixed herself a drink and watched the evening news, glancing at the maddeningly silent phone every few minutes. She managed to hold off until nine o'clock, then lost the battle and dialed Neil's number.

Mrs. Mallory answered and before she could ask for Neil, told her that André was much better, then went on.

"I made him a little stew this evening and he ate all of it, which is more than I can say for my boss. He'll be the death of me yet, fooling around with his food and smoking like a chimney. I heard him pacing around half the night."

"May I speak with him, please?"

"He's working in the den and pulled the phone plug, but if you'll wait, I'll tell him you're on the line."

When Neil answered, his voice was so cold she barely recognized it.

"Yes, Nancy, did you want something?"

"I thought maybe you'd like to come down for a drink."

"No, thanks. I'm working on the Moncrief job. I'm not going into the office for a while, so I had them send over my plans."

Tears welled in Nancy's eyes and she swallowed hard. "Are you trying to tell me you don't want to see me again?"

"No, of course not," Neil said vaguely. "It's just that I've lost a lot of time and have to get on with the job."

"Maybe we could have lunch tomorrow," Nancy suggested, her pride gone.

"Sorry, I have to drive up to Connecticut to tag some more trees and shrubs."

"But it's Saturday. Won't the nurseries be closed?"

"I'm meeting the foreman to go over the stock in the fields."

So he was back in his shell, Nancy thought, and there wasn't much she could do about it. Probably this was the same treatment Bob had gotten the year before. She was almost angry enough to hang up, but still wanted to keep talking to him.

"Mrs. Mallory says André is better," she said.

Neil's tone softened. "Yes, he's doing very well. I didn't have to steer him around the terrace tonight."

She had decided to tell him about seeing Bob, but decided against it.

"Sure you can't come down, darling?" she asked, hating herself for groveling.

"Quite sure, but thank you."

Nancy shoved back her hair with a desperate motion. "Neil, for heaven's sake, stop treating me as though I'm a stranger. I can't stand it."

There was a long pause and she could imagine him at his desk in his shirt sleeves, frowning and probably lighting yet another cigarette.

"Nancy, I tried to explain things to you last night," he said finally. "Nothing has changed and I don't feel free to see you until I know what really happened. You know what I mean."

"And what if the police never solve the case?"

"In that event, I'll go to the inspector and tell him everything I know. I wanted to before, but Andrew wouldn't let me."

Nancy's heart started to hammer. "For God's sake, don't do that, Neil. If you tell the police what you told me last night, they'll hang you."

"Perhaps. I don't really care any more," Neil said wearily. "I'd just like to get the whole damned thing over with."

"Don't you realize that if you go blabbing about Elaine, they'll pin the other murders on you?" Nancy's voice rose. "You must be out of your mind."

"This isn't a matter to discuss on the phone," Neil said, his voice even colder. "Now, if you'll excuse me, I have to get back to work."

There was a click and Nancy was left with a dead line.

She sat there stunned for a moment, then burst into tears. It took her quite a while to pull herself together again and when she did she realized she would have to get help somewhere. She did not really expect Bob's phone to answer and it didn't. He was probably with his girl friend, but if she had ever heard Carol's last name, she didn't remember it.

Andrew, she thought, and, picking up the phone, asked for information. When she finally got her call through, the housekeeper said he was in the city, but she didn't know where. He was meeting a plane and would stay in town all night. Nancy thanked the woman and hung up. The people from London, of course. Andrew would probably take them out on the town and be out late. She tried Kate and Oliver next, hoping that they might be able to influence Neil as she had failed to do, but she could not reach them either. They were helping Andrew entertain his visitors from abroad, no doubt.

Bob seemed to be her best bet, she thought. He had looked tired enough to go home early for once, but the phone did not answer until midnight and after calling every fifteen minutes, she almost fainted when she heard his voice.

"It's Nancy again, Bob," she said. "I talked to Neil tonight and I'm afraid that if someone doesn't stop him, he's going to the police and tell them everything I told you about this afternoon."

"Take it easy, sweetie," Bob said calmly, "and tell me exactly what he said."

Nancy did, pouring it all out in a rush of words, until Bob interrupted her.

"Keep your shirt on, Nancy. He isn't likely to tear down to the police tonight, is he?"

"I don't know what he's going to do, but I thought that if you could talk to him, you might be able to make him see reason."

A deep sigh came over the line; then Bob said, "I couldn't get anywhere with him before. I got the same treatment then that you got tonight."

"Couldn't you go up and see him?"

"He wouldn't see me," Bob said. "Don't forget, I've been through all this before."

"But we've got to do something. He'll hang himself."

"I know, but he won't do anything tonight. I'm sure of that. The only thing I can think of to do is to tell Andrew about it. I'll be seeing him at the office in the morning and I'll tell him the whole thing. Neil probably wouldn't listen to me, but he has great respect for Andrew. Perhaps we can get him down to the office and both go to work on him."

"Bob, I just remembered he said he was going out to Connecticut tomorrow to look at some nursery stock."

"Don't worry. We'll nail him before he leaves."

"Oh, God, I hope so," Nancy said, and then had another thought. "Maybe he isn't planning to go to Connecticut at all, but just said that to get me out of his hair."

"He's probably going if he said he was, but he may be going to get away and think things over before he makes a decision." Bob sounded tired and puzzled. "There's something I don't quite understand."

"What's that?"

"I thought he was nuts about you and that you could influence him, but now he won't even see you. It doesn't make sense."

Nancy gazed across the room, seeing nothing but Neil's handsome, worried face. "I don't think he seriously considered that Elaine might be dead until last night," she said slowly. "He doesn't seem to trust himself. I think he's afraid that if he did those awful things to Elaine, he might do something to another woman he loved."

"Oh, for Christ's sake. He needs a psychiatrist, not a lawyer." Bob seemed angry and impatient, but just as quickly he relented. "Forget that, sweetie. I just hate to see such a swell guy make such an ass of himself."

"I know. I feel the same way. I just wish there were something I could do."

"Maybe there is."

"What?"

"Just don't give up on him. He's lost one woman he loved. Losing another might really send him. He needs you whether he knows it or not."

Nancy came close to crying again, but managed to control herself. "I'll try, Bob, and thanks."

"Now, try and get some sleep."

"Will you let me know how your meeting with Neil turns out, if you can arrange it?"

"Sure thing. Night."

Nancy did not awaken until almost noon the next day. She had tossed and turned and worried for hours, until she had suddenly remembered the two sleeping pills her mother had given her for the plane trip from Rome. She had not needed them, but now she went on a search, found them in her overnight case, gulped them down and fell asleep in no time.

She'd had hours of wonderful oblivion, but woke up feeling groggy and her first thought as she put on the coffee was that Bob might have called while she slept, but the switchboard told her there had been no calls. She had several cups of strong, black coffee, then called the Crawford offices only to find that both Andrew and Bob were still in conference. Miss Hilton did not know when it would be over.

"Will you ask Mr. Crawford to call me back when he's free?" Nancy asked, and left her number. Then she added, "If he is too busy, could you ask Mr. Ewing to call me?"

"Certainly, Miss Gilbert," Miss Hilton said.

It was one-thirty, almost an hour and a half later, before Nancy's phone rang, and by then her nerves were on edge.

She snatched up the receiver. "Bob?"

There was a faint chuckle, then a familiar voice. "No, dear, it's Andrew Crawford."

"Did you see Neil?"

"Yes. Bob told me the whole thing before the conference, so I called Neil and asked him to be here at one to sign some important papers. It worked. When he got here, I talked to him like a Dutch uncle and got him to promise not to do anything until he had given the police a chance to solve the case. We convinced him that it was only fair to Inspector Storm."

"Oh, thank God."

"It's not that great, but he did agree not to make any move until Monday. Now, we can just pray that Storm will come up with something before then."

Nancy hesitated, then decided to ask a question that had been heavily on her mind since Vicky's death.

"Andrew, the inspector seems sure that one of the people who were at Kate and Oliver's is a murderer. Do you think he's right?"

Andrew also hesitated, then said, "Well, from a lawyer's point of view, I think the evidence is pretty thin, as I told him at the time, but even if he is right about Elaine he'll have one hell of a time proving anything unless he has more information than he's told us."

Nancy shuddered. "It's hard to think that someone you know could be a murderer, isn't it?"

"It certainly is." She could almost hear Andrew puffing on his cigar. "Before I forget it, Mrs. Peterson called from Ohio and said Vicky's mother wants André. I'm sorry, but we'll have to arrange for his shipment as soon as he is well enough for the trip."

"Oh, no!" Nancy said, thinking of Mrs. Mallory smiling down at the injured poodle and Neil carrying him to the terrace in his arms as though he were a sick child. She thought of the new dog bowl, the lightweight blanket Mrs. Mallory had bought, the little stews, the lean ground round and André trying so hard to make the best of things, trying to flirt as he had with his mistress before the savage attack on him.

"Don't worry, dear," Andrew said, understanding immediately, "but there's nothing we can do about it."

"Did you tell Neil?"

"No, she only called a few minutes ago and he had already left for Ridgefield."

"Then I'll run up and tell Mrs. Mallory. She's going to be awfully disappointed."

She was about to say good-by and hang up when Andrew spoke again.

"Nancy, Bob told me Neil is refusing to see you and why. Do you want a bit of advice from an old man?"

"Yes, of course."

"Don't let him get away with it. You've got to prove to him somehow that he didn't kill Elaine and wouldn't harm you if his life depended on it."

"All right, I'll try, if I get the chance."

"Good girl."

※※

The day was sunny and mild. Nancy put on a pale blue dress with a matching sweater and set out for the penthouse, stopping on the way to buy a marrow bone at a market. Mrs. Mallory was delighted to see her and led her to the terrace, where André was lying on his blanket, sleeping peacefully.

Mrs. Mallory smiled down at him. "Look who's here, André. It's Miss Gilbert and she's brought you a lovely bone."

André woke up and rolled his eyes while Nancy unwrapped the bone and knelt down beside him. His pom-pom tail wagged and he tried to sit up when Nancy put the bone in front of him. Before he touched it, he gave her hand a little lick, thanking her, then settled down.

"Oh, you darling," Nancy said, and patted his curly head.

Mrs. Mallory was sitting under the garden umbrella, knitting, for all the world like a nanny in Hyde Park on a sunny afternoon. Mike was perched on the table, supervising things, his copper gaze almost paternal.

"Have you had lunch, Miss Gilbert?" Mrs. Mallory asked. "Or perhaps I could fix you something to drink?"

Nancy thought of the news she had to break and decided she could use a tom collins. She had not had any lunch, but the thought of food made her gag. She sat down beside the big poodle, her face pale as she watched him go to work on the bone, delicately at first, then gnawing it happily, looking at her now and then to make sure she was still there.

When Mrs. Mallory returned with her drink, she drank half of it and talked of everything she could think of before she got up the courage to tell the housekeeper the sad news. Mrs. Mallory had black hair, which was probably dyed, a gentle, round face and eyes as blue as Neil's. They stared at her for a moment, then filled with tears. She had stopped knitting and her plump hands were idle in her lap.

It occurred to Nancy that during her years of domestic service the poor woman must have had to part with many pets she had grown to love in other people's houses and was probably lucky that she could hang on to her cat.

"I'm terribly sorry, Mrs. Mallory," she said.

The housekeeper shook her head sadly. "I don't know when I've gotten so fond of a dog in such a short time. He's such a lovely little fellow." She sighed deeply and picked up her knitting. "Mr. Stratton loves him too. Maybe it's because he seemed to need us so much."

Nancy looked down at André and swallowed a lump in her throat. He cast her a merry glance and went on crunching happily.

"Did Mr. Stratton say when he would be home?" she asked.

"No, but he will be home for dinner. He always tells me if he won't be. He's always so thoughtful about things like that." Mrs. Mallory's voice was strained and she threw her knitting to the table. "Excuse me, miss, but I have to fix André's eggnog now. We're trying to build him up, you see."

Nancy kissed the top of André's head and got up. "Don't worry about me, Mrs. Mallory. I'll see myself out."

But the housekeeper was already on her way into the penthouse, her small, plump body very erect, her head high, obviously trying to control herself until she got to the privacy of her own quarters, where she could let go. Mike jumped off the table and trotted after her.

For the first time in her life Nancy used Bobo Babson's favorite word, then picked up her purse and fled, afraid that if she looked back at André, she would go to pieces.

She walked over to Lexington Avenue, bought a newspaper at a drugstore and ordered a ham sandwich and coffee. She read the apartments-for-rent ads while she forced down the sandwich, but all she could think of was André, so secure in his new home, and as happy as he could be under the circumstances. Finally, she put the paper down and went to a phone booth, where she looked up the Crawford firm's number again, and again she got Miss Hilton.

"Is Mr. Crawford still there?" Nancy asked.

"Oh, I'm so glad you called," Miss Hilton said. "I just missed you at Mr. Stratton's. Mr. Crawford wants to see you. Can you come down to the office?"

"Yes, I'll be right down," Nancy said. "I want to see him, too."

"Because it's the weekend you'll have to sign in downstairs and most of our people have gone for the day, so I will meet you at the elevator."

❦

In sharp contrast to Vicky's blond roundness, Andrew's new secretary was tall and thin with dark hair, cut short.

"I'm Madge Hilton," she said as Nancy stepped out of the elevator. "If you'll come this way, please. Mr. Crawford is waiting for you."

Nancy followed her down a large hall, into a lavish, empty reception room, then down another hall, this one heavily carpeted, and nodded toward a mahogany door at the end.

"Do you know why he wants to see me?" Nancy asked, a little awed by the lavish offices and solemn atmosphere.

Miss Hilton smiled, as though humoring a child. "You'll find out soon enough." She went on to the door and opened it.

"Miss Gilbert is here, Mr. Crawford," she said, and quickly withdrew.

As Nancy went in, Andrew got up to meet her, beaming and waving his eternal cigar. "I'm so glad you could come, my dear."

He seated Nancy in a leather chair, then returned to his own seat behind his desk, put down his cigar and picked up a letter.

"This just came in a little while ago," he said. "It's a Special Delivery Air Mail from your Uncle George. He wants you to have the beach house in Westport."

Nancy stared at him. "But it's Elaine's."

Andrew shook his head and picked up his cigar. "When George and his wife were divorced, the terms were that she would have the use of the property for as long as she lived, then it would go to Elaine, but if they both predeceased him, it would revert back to him, unless Elaine had legal heirs, which she didn't."

"But I don't want it," Nancy said, horrified. "I used to love it, but now I never want to see it again."

"Oh, come now," Andrew said, smiling. "Don't let sentiment stand in your way. It's an extremely valuable property and if you don't want it yourself, you can rent it or sell it for a very good price. Waterfront property is sky-high and you could get enough to provide a good income for years, if it's properly invested."

Nancy brushed aside her bangs, looking bewildered. "But Elaine hasn't even been declared legally dead. How can Uncle George give it to me?"

"There is a contingency clause in the contract stating that

he would pay the taxes and insurance, in return for which he would retain title to the property. It was his intention to leave it outright to Elaine when he died, but now the circumstances have changed and he wants you to have it immediately to do with as you please." Andrew pushed the letter across the desk. "Read it yourself."

She did and found that everything Andrew said was true, but he had omitted a postscript at the bottom.

"I'm afraid I won't be around very much longer, and I would like to have the matter settled before I die," Uncle George had written. "I never trusted Elaine or her mother with financial matters, but I'm sure my little niece will use the property wisely. With kindest personal regards, George Parker."

"Oh, Lord," Nancy said, handing back the letter and shrinking back in the big leather chair.

"You'll hurt him dreadfully if you don't accept," Andrew wheedled. "Elaine's been such a disappointment to him and he seems to have put you in her place."

"But he has two sons . . ."

"Don't worry about them. They'll be well provided for. He's a very wealthy man. The point is, he wants *you* to have the property." Andrew's pale eyes met hers. "It would be downright mean of you to refuse him."

Nancy shrank back even further, her mind in a whirl. As a child she had often visited the beach house with her mother and had loved the airiness of the house and its setting overlooking the water and the beach. It had been well kept then and nicely decorated with appointments suggesting the sea. But now all she could think of was Elaine in Neil's strong arms and the heaven he had enjoyed there before it turned to hell. She recoiled from the thought.

Andrew, as though reading her mind, pointed to a legal-looking document on his desk with his cigar.

"You might as well agree to it now. That's George's new

will. If you won't accept the place as a gift, you'll get it any-way. He has left it to you and there will be a stiff inheritance tax." Andrew's shrewd lawyer eyes gleamed at the prospect of snatching money from the greedy jaws of the govern-ment. "Shall I go ahead and draw up the necessary papers?"

"I guess there isn't much choice," Nancy said reluctantly.

"Good girl." Andrew was beaming again. "I happen to know a little of your financial situation, my dear, and a steady income never hurt a woman. You'll be glad of it all your life."

He got up, as though in a hurry to get rid of Nancy before she changed her mind. She got up too, but instead of leaving she looked at Andrew gravely.

"Do you know Mrs. Colton's address?" she asked.

Andrew looked startled, then frowned. "She lives in some suburb outside Akron with a funny name Vicky used to joke about. Can't think of it now."

"Never mind, I'll ask Bob on the way out."

"He's left for the day." Andrew raised his silver eyebrows. "May I ask what you want with Vicky's mother?"

"Yes, that's what I wanted to see you about. I want to ask her if she will sell André to me, so that I can give him to Neil and Mrs. Mallory."

"Oh, I wouldn't do that, if I were you," Andrew said, frowning again. "Besides, I believe she is still in the hos-pital."

"I know, but she and Mrs. Peterson live together and I thought I could ask Mrs. Peterson to give her the message for me."

Andrew shrugged and pushed a button on his intercom. Miss Hilton's voice came through instantly. "Yes, Mr. Crawford?"

"See if you can find the address of Mrs. Colton. She's Vicky's mother. Personnel is closed, of course, but look in Bob's office. He may have it there."

Andrew turned to Nancy. "Why André? If Neil wants a poodle, he can certainly afford to go out and buy one for himself."

"You don't understand," Nancy said with a sad smile. "He and Mrs. Mallory are nuts about André."

"Well, I think it's very bad taste to ask for the dog at a time like this." Andrew's tanned face was stern with disapproval. "She may feel obligated to sell him if you give her a sob story, and she might want him badly because he was Vicky's. But suit yourself."

"I guess you're right," Nancy said, and swallowed another lump in her throat.

Miss Hilton's cool voice came over the intercom. "It's Mrs. Bertha Colton, Twenty-seven Walnut Street, LeRoy, Ohio, sir. Shall I bring it in?"

"No, thanks, Madge. We won't need it now."

Andrew led Nancy to the door, opened it and his stern expression turned to a smile. "Why don't you take a run up to Westport and have a look at the place? I haven't been there in years, but I understand Elaine and her mother let it run down and you will want to put it in good condition no matter what you do with it." Andrew reached out a pudgy hand and patted her shoulder. "Don't worry about the expense. I'll advance you any amount you need to get it in shape."

"Thank you, Andrew," Nancy said dubiously. "I'll have to think it over."

"No time like the present to get things done. When you get to be my age you realize that." Andrew reached into his pocket and came up with a set of keys on a small metal chain. Attached to it was a cardboard tag saying, "Parker, Westport."

"I dug these up while I was waiting for you. We've had to send someone out there from time to time to check on the place for the insurance people. Elaine and her mother were so sloppy about things that George worried about it."

Nancy took them and dropped them into her purse.

"Good luck with it, dear," Andrew said.

She nodded and left him standing in the doorway, waving good-by with his cigar and smiling, obviously pleased with himself.

Feeling lonely and more depressed than ever, Nancy stopped to do some marketing, then returned to her apartment, where she moped around and tried again to concentrate on the new book, but it was hopeless. Then the phone rang. This time she did not allow herself to hope it would be Neil, so she was not too disappointed when she heard Kate Vail's pleasant voice on the line.

"Dad just phoned and told us about the beach house," she said gaily. "It's great! I've always thought it could be a fabulous place if it were done up right. Oliver and I have to go to an art exhibit later, but why don't you pop up and have a drink to celebrate. Bob Ewing is coming for dinner. Perhaps you could join us if you haven't other plans. Dad says Neil is somewhere in Connecticut looking at trees."

"That's all he seems to do. Trees or shrubs or plans for that damned job."

Kate laughed. "Then Bob can be your dinner partner. His girl friend's husband is in town and he's afraid to go near her. Paul Kendell is bringing Bobo for a drink and they're staying for dinner too. We'll have a nice little party."

"Thanks, Kate, I'd love to come."

"At sixish, darling."

Which in New York meant six-thirty, Nancy thought, and took her time changing into a sea-green cocktail dress with matching wool coat she'd had made by a little dressmaker in Paris. Before she left, she gave Kate's number to the switchboard operator in case Neil should call. Probably a waste of time, but he was so moody and unpredictable anything might happen.

⨯

Kate, who apparently thought a party could improve any situation, no matter how desperate, had managed to create a cheerful atmosphere. There were flowers all over the big living room, a hidden stereo was playing soft background music, and Oliver was behind the bar, wearing his maroon dinner jacket, his friendly, battered face animated as he took orders from his guests.

Bob and Paul and Bobo were already there when Nancy arrived, and Kate came toward her, flashing her broad smile.

"I'm so glad you could come, dear, and it's just wonderful about the beach house. Come and tell Oliver what you would like to drink."

She led Nancy to the bar, where the others were drinking and chattering, so nonchalant that it seemed incredible that their last meeting there had been called to advise them of Elaine's death. Looking around the group she could see no sign of worry, guilt or even distress on any face.

Bob got off a barstool and greeted her, and so did Paul Kendell, but Bobo gave her a brief, green stare and a little nod. Oliver leaned over the bar. "I know," he said jovially. "A martini, very dry."

"Yes, thanks." Nancy chose a stool and Bob perched on the one next to it.

"It's swell about your getting the beach house. Elaine never seemed to give a damn about it, but I bet you can do wonders with it." He took out a pack of cigarettes and offered it to her.

She took one and frowned while he lit it for her. "I'm not sure I want it after all that's happened there."

"Sweetie, you need a manager. That place could be worth a fortune." He lit his own cigarette and snapped his lighter shut. "Besides, how do you know what happened there? Maybe nothing at all."

"But Inspector Storm thinks . . ."

"That's just it, he *thinks*." Bob cut in. "He hasn't a shred of real evidence, just a lousy suitcase some kid found." He shrugged. "Hell, for all we know Elaine could have left it at the beach house when she took off after her fight with Neil. By the way, where is he? Still in his shell?"

"I guess he's home now. He went out to Connecticut, but Mrs. Mallory expects him back for dinner." Speaking of Neil made her feel uneasy, so she changed the subject. "Are you going to the exhibit?"

Bob smiled and suddenly looked young and very attractive and his dark eyes sparkled behind his glasses.

"Good God, no. It's a one-man show Kate is sponsoring and they're always fatal." He laughed. "For the first time in months I'm going home early and get some sleep. I'm crazy about Carol, but she never wants to go to bed . . . I mean she can sleep until noon and she doesn't care when . . ."

He floundered on until Nancy said, "Never mind, I get the picture."

Kate had moved off to join Bobo and Paul at the other end of the bar and Nancy noticed with amusement that Kate with her tall, well-built body made Bobo look as though she might expire at any moment. Her blond hair was piled on top of her head and her emaciated figure was encased in another sheath, a gray one this time, and her long silver earrings swung when she moved her head. The scent of her heavy perfume hung in the air, mixing with the cigarette smoke, creating a sort of sophisticated smog.

"Well, I'll be damned," Bob said.

Nancy turned back to him and, following the direction of his startled gaze, saw the maid taking Andrew's hat and a tall brunette's stole. The woman was Miss Hilton, who must have gone home to change and was now wearing a smart black dinner dress.

Bob grinned impishly. "I didn't think she was his type."

Andrew guided Miss Hilton to the bar, introduced her and beamed at them all.

"Madge has just come on from Chicago and doesn't know many people here," he explained. "So I thought I would ask her to dinner with us."

The Vails did not seem at all surprised. After all, they had known Vicky well and were used to Andrew's ways. Kate made the secretary welcome and Oliver smiled and wielded his bar cloth.

"Let me guess," he said, appraising Madge Hilton's clean-cut features and neatly trimmed dark hair, then snapping his fingers. "I know. A vodka martini."

Miss Hilton laughed and shook her head. "Nothing, thanks. I don't drink."

A sudden silence fell on the group, as though Miss Hilton had announced that she was Typhoid Mary.

Oliver's smile died and Kate seemed stunned, then said, "What about some ginger ale, dear, or perhaps a lemonade?"

"Or a nice cold beer, maybe?" Oliver asked, as though the thought of a guest in his home without a glass of something was inconceivable.

"Ginger ale would be fine," Miss Hilton said, and settled down on a barstool, cool and composed and apparently unaware of the sensation she had caused. The stool she had chosen was on the other side of Bob's and she started talking to him. He turned to her, leaving Nancy alone until Andrew came up behind her, reached over her shoulder for the drink Oliver made for him and coughed.

"Excuse me, dear," he said.

Nancy thought he would sit on the empty stool on her right, but when she turned to him, he was still standing there, sampling his drink and looking at her as though he had an amusing secret to tell her.

"You look pleased about something," she said.

"I am. I've been thinking about your wanting to buy Vicky's dog and I've come up with a solution."

Nancy smiled eagerly. "Then you think it's all right if I call Ohio? You've changed your mind?"

Andrew shook his head. "No, I don't mean that, but if Neil and Mrs. Mallory are so fond of André, I thought it might be a good idea to go to the breeder I got him from. She's a Mrs. Gordon and she has a show kennel near my place in Greenwich."

"That's sweet of you," Nancy said, trying to cover her disappointment, "but you don't understand. It's André they've fallen for."

"But we could probably get a pup with the same bloodlines." Andrew took a sip of his drink and regarded her hopefully. "Be like André. Don't you see?"

All Nancy could see was André being crated and hauled away to strangers in Ohio and Neil and Mrs. Mallory being forced to watch the ordeal helplessly.

"No," she said stubbornly. "It has to be André or nothing."

"But you promised you wouldn't try to buy him," Andrew insisted.

"I didn't promise anything." Her eyes, meeting his, were getting colder by the moment. "You said you thought it was poor taste to call at a time like this and I said maybe you were right, but I didn't say anything about later, when Mrs. Colton is well."

"You're nit-picking and you certainly implied . . ."

Nancy cocked her head to one side and her chin went up. "Maybe she'll find she's not up to taking care of a dog after she gets out of the hospital. Or she might just change her mind."

Andrew looked annoyed. "Why should she change her mind? She wants the dog and that's that."

"Well, I could at least let her know someone wants him if it doesn't work out, and I intend to do just that," Nancy said, and swung her stool around, turning her back on him. She was being rude, but she was too polite to tell him she didn't think it was any of his damned business and he was the one who was interfering.

Andrew shrugged and went off to join his daughter at the other end of the bar.

Oliver paused in the midst of adding a shot to his own drink and mockingly shook his index finger at her. "Mustn't argue with Papa, you know. He's used to getting his own way."

"It doesn't pay to argue with any lawyer," a voice on Nancy's right said, and turning, she was surprised to see that Paul Kendell was sitting there looking at her with a glint of amusement in his pale blue eyes. He was wearing a dark suit and an orange tie that made his hair look like tight carrot curls.

"Don't you know that lawyers and presidents think they're gods, darling," he added, and turned to Oliver. "What she needs is another drink."

Oliver's friendly face lit up. "Doesn't everybody?"

Paul Kendell sat smoking and drinking thoughtfully, but Oliver, the perfect host adept at handling people, brushed off the incident by telling her a funny story and by the time the maid announced dinner, she was completely over her brief fit of anger. The gin had given her a happy glow and she had even forgotten her worry about Neil when Bob took her in to dinner.

The dining room, like everything else at the Vails' was beautifully appointed, the walls done in sky blue to match the Wedgwood service, the table gay with flowers, crystal glasses and soft candlelight.

Although Kate was meticulous about the food she served at her smaller dinners, she was not fussy about the seating arrangements. She put Madge on her left and Andrew on her right, while Nancy found herself on Oliver's right at his end of the table, between him and Bob. Paul was on Oliver's left, across from her and Bobo beside him.

There was green turtle soup, filet of sole, roast lamb, fresh vegetables, crisp salad and a variety of wines for each course. A trim maid poured the wine with the ease of a sommelier. The conversation was bright, the atmosphere gay and everything so pleasant that it was difficult to believe that underneath it all there was tension.

Nancy began to feel it, but it did not surface until they were nearing the end of dinner and one of the maids came in and whispered something to her mistress; then Kate looked down the table to Nancy.

"A call for you, dear. It's Mrs. Mallory," she said. "Alice will show you where to take it."

Nancy got up and followed the maid to a room off the hall, a sort of feminine office which Kate probably used to do her household accounts, plan menus and make private phone calls. There was an antiqued white desk, a matching chair, a chaise and a few other chairs. The phone was also white, and as Nancy picked it up, she wondered if it was from here that Vicky had made her call to Neil just before her death.

She waited until the maid had left, then said, "Yes, Mrs. Mallory?"

There was a sound almost like a sob, and the housekeeper gasped, "Oh, thank God, I got you. It's Mr. Stratton, miss. He phoned a few minutes ago to say he wouldn't be home to dinner. It's twenty minutes past eight and I've been trying to hold dinner."

Nancy frowned, wondering why Mrs. Mallory was so upset. "He must have been held up somewhere," she said. "Nothing to worry about."

"But he's always let me know if there would be any change in plans, and that's not all, Miss Gilbert, it's the way he talked. I've been worried about the way he's been acting lately, not like himself at all, as though something is preying on his mind."

"I know."

"And when I asked him when he would be home, he said he didn't know. He sounded so queer." Mrs. Mallory's voice rose. "Like he was drunk or doped or something. It was hard to understand him, but I think he said he was going to meet Elaine."

"*Elaine!*" Nancy slumped into the small white chair and ran her fingers through her hair. "Are you sure, Mrs. Mallory? The police think she's dead, you know."

"Yes, I know, that's why I'm so frightened."

Nancy's knuckles were white as she clutched the receiver. "Did he say where he was?"

"That was funny, too," Mrs. Mallory said frantically. "When I asked him, he said something about going to West Point. Now, what would he be going there for?"

Westport, Nancy thought, her heart thumping. She wanted to scream, but the housekeeper's near hysteria forced her to seem calm.

"Listen, Mrs. Mallory, you just stay there and try not to worry. I'll get away from here as soon as I can without attracting too much attention, and . . ."

"Shouldn't we call the police? I'm so afraid he might . . ."

"No, don't call anybody. Just sit tight and if he should call again, try to keep him talking."

"What are you going to do, miss?"

"Try to find him."

"Oh, merciful God!" Mrs. Mallory cried, and then her voice trailed off in a burst of sobs as she hung up.

Nancy put the white receiver back on its cradle and stared at it, her mind clicking like a time bomb; then she got up, squared her shoulders and returned to the dining room, her head high, her face deathly pale.

The maid was serving strawberries in crystal bowls and Kate at her end of the table was pouring coffee into small cups, while Oliver was presiding over a tray of liqueurs.

"We're going to have coffee in here tonight," Kate said, glancing up at Nancy and smiling. "Because of the exhibit, you know. Jimmie will be furious if we're . . . Why, Nancy, what's the matter? You look like a ghost."

Nancy forced an answering smile as she went back to her seat and slipped into it. But Kate wasn't to be put off. She lowered the silver coffee pot and looked straight at Nancy.

"Has something happened to Neil?" she asked.

"No, nothing important." Nancy sat very straight and her luminous eyes were expressionless. "Mrs. Mallory was just worried because he didn't come home for dinner."

"That *is* odd," Kate said with a small frown as she went on pouring. "He's always so good about being on time for meals. Mrs. Mallory is always boasting about it. I hope nothing's wrong."

Nancy shrugged. "He might have had car trouble or something."

She tried to sound elaborately casual, but her voice came out strained and hollow. She looked around to see if she had managed to fool the others. Bob was sipping his demitasse and chatting with Madge Hilton, and Oliver, on her other side, was looking at her inquiringly, which startled her for a second before he spoke.

"I asked if you would rather have a brandy or a liqueur," he said. "This is excellent Rémy Martin."

She didn't want anything, but she accepted the cognac, determined to make things seem normal and not to arouse suspicion. She was doggedly finishing her strawberries when she became aware of Paul Kendell's pale blue eyes trained on her, bright in the candlelight. She turned away and saw Bobo regarding her with a green stare over the rim of her liqueur glass. It took her a minute to realize that Bobo was quite tight and the stare glassy.

Nancy, continuing her round, saw that Andrew was telling some long-winded story to his daughter and Madge Hilton. She could not see the secretary's face, but Kate wasn't listening. She was looking straight at Nancy, her brown eyes worried and knowing.

She was still looking at Nancy when she suddenly put her napkin on the table and got up. "It's been fun, but Oliver and I must get started if we're going to be at Jimmie's show on time." Her warm smile swept around the table, including them all. This must have been the way she had gotten rid of her guests the evening Vicky had been killed, Nancy thought.

"Suits me," Andrew said. "It's been a tough day and I want to get back to Greenwich."

Everyone got up as though royalty had spoken and as they trailed out of the dining room, Kate hung back, waiting for Nancy.

"Something's wrong, isn't it?" she asked, putting her hand on Nancy's arm. "Why, you're trembling."

Nancy looked into Kate's dark eyes and decided she had to trust her. She had thought of renting a car, but remembered that she had not renewed her driving license and a taxi was out of the question, even if she could find one willing to drive her to Westport.

Kate's hand tightened on her arm. "Is it Neil?"

"Yes." Nancy hesitated, then went on, praying that she was doing the right thing. "He called Mrs. Mallory and told her he was on his way to Westport. She thought he sounded drunk."

"Oh, good Lord."

"Have you a car I could borrow?"

"Yes, of course, but are you sure you should go alone?"

Nancy nodded. "He's not rational. He thinks he might have killed Elaine and that he might hurt me. I want to prove to him that he couldn't hurt anybody and never has."

"Oh, Nancy." Kate looked troubled. "I don't think I should let you . . ."

"You'll have to, Kate. If I don't get there soon I might be too late. He told Mrs. Mallory he was going to see Elaine. He might . . ." Nancy gulped and tears sprang up in her eyes.

"All right, dear. You wait in the living room. I'll call the garage and have my car sent around."

Nancy watched her go into the small, feminine office, then went on into the living room. There was a small powder room off it and she went to freshen up before the long drive. When she came out Bob joined her and asked if he could take her home.

"No, thanks, Bob," she said. "It's miles out of your way. I can catch a cab."

"Then I'll run along." Bob smiled, then went to thank his hostess, who was in the hall bidding her father and Miss Hilton good-by.

Oliver, again behind the bar, was making a quick, final drink. Bobo, swaying on a barstool, was his only customer until Paul came from somewhere, carrying a slinky black fur jacket.

"No reason for you people to leave," Oliver said. "Stick around and have more drinks if you like. Just because we have to go to this damned thing . . ."

"Thanks, Oliver," Paul said, slipping the jacket over Bobo's shoulders, "but I have to get my friend home while she can still walk."

He managed to get Bobo into her jacket and raised his

eyes to heaven as he guided her out, holding her upright while he stopped to chat for a moment with Kate. When everyone else had gone, Kate came over to the bar, where Nancy was waiting with Oliver, who seemed a little puzzled that she was still there.

"Nancy is waiting for my car," Kate explained, keeping her tone light. "Seems Neil's cockeyed out in Westport and she wants to go get him."

Oliver frowned and downed the rest of his brandy. "I thought something was wrong, but what in hell is Neil doing in Westport? He's always sworn he'd never go near the place again."

"That, darling, is none of our business," Kate said. "Now, run and take off that horrible jacket and get into something respectable."

"All this for a queer who paints soup cans and garbage pails," Oliver said, but he left.

The minute he was gone, Kate turned to Nancy. "Do be careful, dear," she said anxiously. "If anything happens to you, I'll never forgive myself."

Nancy's chin went up. "Don't worry, Kate. Nothing's going to happen to me. I'll be safe with Neil."

Kate seemed to waver, then told Nancy there was a flashlight in the glove compartment if she needed it. The keys to the beach house were still in Nancy's purse, because she had forgotten to take them out, so she was ready to leave when the maid finally came in to tell them the car was waiting.

It had been years since Nancy had driven out to the beach house, but she remembered that she and her mother had always avoided the truck-laden routes along the shore of the Sound, using instead the West Side Highway, the Saw Mill, then turning off for the Merritt Parkway.

Kate's car was a Buick, much heavier and larger than

anything she had driven in Europe, but the garage attendant, who had brought the car, showed her how to operate it
and she got the hang of it by the time she got to the Merritt.
From then on, she had no trouble. The car purred along
the wide rolling parkway and it was pleasant to see trees
again if only by the headlights. The weekend traffic was
light and she drove as fast as she dared with no license. It
seemed an eternity before she saw the sign on her right
pointing to Westport.

A couple of miles further on, she came to the town and
then got hopelessly lost. Like almost every other place
on earth, it had grown and changed, but she remembered
the Marina which Inspector Storm had mentioned and
knowing that if she could get there, she could find her way
to the beach house, she stopped at a gas station for
directions.

"Go down to the second traffic light, then turn left and
keep going. You can't miss it," the man told her.

Probably because it was Saturday, there was a gaiety
about the place. Stores were lit up and houses glowed in-
vitingly. There were apartments which had not been there
before and other new buildings, but as she got nearer the
shore, there was a more subdued atmosphere. She slowed
down when she saw the Marina ahead, then turned left into
the old beach road.

There were more new houses, some of them with lights
and others closed for the season. It was a cloudy night with
a stiff breeze blowing in from the Sound and she could hear
the surf pounding on the beach. As she passed the last house
before the Parker property, she saw that it was boarded up
and grew more nervous. When she finally pulled off the
road, her throat was dry and her heart pounding.

There had once been a seashell drive to the house, but
now it was covered with sand and she was afraid of getting
stuck in it, so she parked on the edge of the road, got out

the keys Andrew had given her and Kate's flashlight before turning off the headlights; then she got out and stood by the car until her eyes adjusted to the darkness.

The cold breeze whipped her hair and went through her lightweight coat. Overhead, the sky was filled with running clouds playing hide-and-seek with a far-off moon. As her eyes became accustomed to the gloom, she could make out the beach house, foreboding and lonely with only a few scrub pines, sand and clumps of tall grass around it.

She decided against using the flashlight and to have a look around before she went into the house. As she picked her way through the sand, the moon emerged from behind the clouds and her nervousness increased. There was no sign of life anywhere, just the brooding gray shingle house, the surf pounding behind it and the wind lashing at the grass. A loose shutter squealed from an upper window as it swung crazily from its broken hinges.

She was so intent on getting to Neil that she was halfway around the house before it occurred to her that something was wrong. If Neil were there, why wasn't his car up on the road where she had parked the Buick? Had he hidden it somewhere, or had he been there and gone? Assuming that he had been drunk, as Mrs. Mallory suspected, he might have sobered up and changed his mind, but that was not like Neil.

She squared her shoulders and kept on and before the moon went behind the dark clouds again, she saw the mounds of sand where the police had been digging, looking for Elaine's body. The thought terrified her, but she kept on. Neil had said he was going to see Elaine, which could only mean one thing. He planned to kill himself. No longer able to cope with the mess she had made of his life, he was going to join her in death.

And if Inspector Storm was right, Elaine was out there in the dark, angry waters of the Sound, her bones weighed down with concrete blocks. The thought sent her running around the corner of the house, her high heels sinking in the sand, until she stopped and kicked them off.

There was an incline where the house ended and the sun deck began. Below, she could see the beach with the rioting surf pounding against it, advancing and receding with a roaring rhythm. She stumbled down the incline and then stopped as she reached the beach. The wind whipped against her while she waited for the moon to emerge again.

When it did, she went on, running parallel to the foaming surf, her frightened eyes scanning the wet sand; then suddenly she could see the dock where Neil was supposed to have tried to drown her cousin. It appeared to be deserted and as she ran closer she could see that the tide must be low, because the waves were well below it, swirling around the pilings. Was Neil's body swirling around them too?

She ran on, feeling splinters dig into her feet as she reached the dock's weather-worn boards, then slowed down as she realized that some of the planks were rotten. It was agony to pick her way and she was exhausted by the time she came to the end and stood with the wind even fiercer, tearing at her hair and whipping her thin coat around her legs. She stared down at the dark, murky waves, as though hypnotized, then realized that it was insane to stand there any longer.

Neil wouldn't expect that she or anyone else would come to interfere with his plans. He could be up in the dark house, brooding, or drinking, or even passed out. With the keys clutched in one hand and Kate's flashlight in the other, she started to turn back, then froze as she realized she wasn't alone. Someone was standing behind her, someone who was breathing so hard she could hear it over the pulsing of the waves.

She stood, too petrified to move; then as she whirled around, she felt hands grab her by the neck. She dropped the

keys and the flashlight and tried to pull the tightening fingers
from her throat, but they were holding her in a vice, so that
she couldn't turn to see their owner, but she knew as she
struggled that it was someone tall and strong, because of
the angle of the hands and their strength.

Oh, God, she thought, it couldn't be Neil, but who else
could it be? Then she heard the sound of heavy footsteps
on the old planks and men's voices. The hands let go of her
and she dropped in a heap on the dock, panting, trying to
get her breath; then someone reached down to help her up.

"Are you all right, Miss Gilbert?"

It took her several minutes to realize that there were other
men there and that it was Inspector Storm's voice.

"Yes, I'm all right," she said, rubbing her throat and turning around toward the house.

Two men with flashlights were leading a figure down the
dock and then the lights in the house suddenly went on, as
if on signal, and to her horror she could see that the figure
was tall and dark and the men on either side of it were in
uniforms of some kind.

Inspector Storm indicated a man next to him. "This is
Lieutenant Craig of the Connecticut State Police, Miss Gilbert," he said, then nodded toward the other man. "And
you remember Sergeant Romano, of course."

Nancy didn't look at either of them. She just kept staring
at the figure, now being led across the sand and up the steps
to the sun deck, going along quietly as though knowing that
all hope was gone, everything over.

"How did you know he was going to come here?" she
asked.

"We have our methods," the inspector said.

She turned to him as he spoke and saw that he was
standing there like a soldier at attention, even with the wind
blowing his hair and flapping his coat. But the appalling
thing about it was that even in the dim moonlight she could

see that he seemed to be smiling, looking smug and pleased with himself.

She felt sick and, for the first time in her life, came near fainting.

Inspector Storm reached out and took hold of her. "I know this must have been horrible for you," he said, his smile gone. "Come, we'll go up to the house."

She went along numbly, her mind a blank until they reached the steps leading up to the sun deck, where the men paused as if waiting for something. Then the two men in uniforms of the Connecticut State Police came out to the sun deck and down the steps to join them.

There was a short conference; then Lieutenant Craig said, "Well, I guess you and your men can take it from here, Inspector. They are all there."

The inspector thanked them for their co-operation and the three men went off, circling the house.

Nancy looked up at the broad steps and drew back. "I don't want to go up there," she said frantically. "Can't I just go back to New York?"

"No, I'm afraid not." The inspector frowned. "You surprise me. I thought you would be glad that we have apprehended the person who was responsible for your cousin's death and the murder of two other innocent people."

Nancy suddenly thought of Elaine's beautiful body rotting in the sea, and friendly, plump little Vicky brutally strangled and a poor reporter mugged and murdered, leaving a wife and kids behind to suffer. And then she thought of André savagely kicked and bruised and she turned to the inspector, her eyes bright with fear and anger.

"You've got the wrong man," she said. "Neil could never have done these terrible things."

"Neil?" Storm's mouth dropped open, then broke into a wide smile. "Neil is probably on his way from the state police barracks by now. We had to hold him there for fear he would louse up everything. We had a hell of a time getting him to go along with our plan."

Nancy shook her head, bewildered. "I don't understand."

"You will soon enough," the inspector said, and led her up the steps.

When they reached the big sun deck, she could see the living room through the expanse of mullioned windows on either side of the door. It was a large room with several tired old sofas and chairs and the long picnic table where Nancy remembered eating during her long-ago summer visits and where Elaine had written her poems on rainy days.

She stopped short, gazing into the room, seeing several men she had never seen before, probably detectives from Storm's Homicide Department, and others who shouldn't be there at all. Kate was sitting on one of the old blue sofas, between her father and Miss Hilton, and Oliver was standing off to one side, next to one of the strange men, his usually friendly face stiff and strained. On another sofa, Paul Kendell sat staring straight in front of him, ignoring the man beside him. Bob Ewing was in a chair by himself, but she could only see his head and shoulders because of the tattered blue curtains covering part of the right windows.

"How did they get here?" Nancy asked.

"Our men brought them out in police cars and held them down the road until the signal."

"But why?"

"Because it was easier to bring them here to put the pieces together than to question them individually later in the city with the press on our backs."

Nancy's glance went to Andrew's new secretary, who was sitting quietly beside Kate. "That's Miss Hilton," she said. "What could she . . . ?"

"She's a policewoman."

They moved forward and Sergeant Romano went ahead to open the door. It was not until they were in the room that Nancy saw to her horror that one of the people in it wore handcuffs and it had to be the person who had just tried to murder her. She couldn't believe it, but as she went further into the room, the figure raised his head and their eyes met.

It was Bob Ewing.

He didn't say anything, but simply stared at her. She stared back until Inspector Storm gently escorted her to a wicker love seat that she remembered out on the sun deck years before. It still had the same blue and white cushions, white sails against a blue sea. She collapsed on it, threw her head back and closed her eyes. The numbness was wearing off, leaving her in a state bordering on shock. People were talking, but she didn't hear what they were saying and didn't care. Then she felt a hand touch her shoulder, and, opening her eyes, saw Oliver Vail leaning over her, holding out a silver flask and a jelly glass.

"I smuggled in some brandy," he said, pouring a stiff shot. "Knock it off fast before they pinch me."

She took it and gulped down most of it and it felt wonderful going down, warming and comforting. The cold terror began to subside and it eased her quivering stomach. Oliver waited until she had finished, then took the glass and as he left she saw Kate coming toward her with an anxious smile.

"I've been so damned worried, darling," she said. "I didn't want to let them risk your life, but it was the only way . . . I didn't tell Oliver the truth until after you had left, because he would never have let you go. Can you ever forgive me?"

"Of course," Nancy said, "but I don't know what for."

Inspector Storm suddenly took command and even though his suit was wrinkled and his silvery brown hair mussed from the wind, his gray eyes were alert. He was standing by the empty stone fireplace, where he could easily see around the room.

"Will you please return to your seat, Mrs. Vail," he said. "You can talk among yourselves later."

Nancy watched Kate meekly return to her place on the sofa with her father and Madge Hilton and then she noticed a man sitting on a bench at the picnic table. Sergeant Romano was across from him and between them was something she had never seen before except on television, a tape recorder. It was open and they were doing something to it, and the sergeant kept glancing at his boss as though waiting for some kind of signal.

The front door was suddenly flung open and Neil strode in, looking tired and angry and handsome. He was wearing a tweed jacket and slacks and his blue eyes were flashing as he went toward Bob. One of the men who had been standing by the door moved forward, but a look from the inspector stopped him. Then as Neil reached Bob and stood in front of him, Storm nodded to his sergeant.

"How could you, Bob?" Neil said. "Jesus Christ, how could you? I couldn't really believe it until they told me they'd trapped you."

Bob looked up at him and his dark eyes behind his glasses were hostile. "It all started because I was trying to protect you."

Neil looked bewildered. "From what?"

"From Elaine," Bob said angrily. "If it hadn't been for your goddamned money . . ."

Bob's mouth clamped shut. Neil seemed too stunned to speak, then turned and looked around the room until he spotted Nancy. He hurried over to her.

"Darling, I was against all this and I thought Inspector Storm was crazy. They had a tail on me and he caught up with me at the nurseries in Ridgefield. Are you all right?"

"Yes, but I wish I knew what was going on," Nancy said, and when he sat down beside her she had a wild impulse to fling herself into his arms.

Andrew Crawford suddenly leaned forward and looked at Inspector Storm. "Let's get on with this, sir. My daughter and I have done everything you required of us, which was most unpleasant, but before you begin, have you warned Bob that he doesn't have to answer any questions which might . . . ?"

"Yes, Mr. Crawford, we have, and I would like to remind you that this isn't a courtroom and Robert Ewing is not under oath. We have suspected him for some time, but there are still some questions that have to be answered before our investigation is complete. That's why I brought you here."

"What made you suspect Bob?" Andrew asked, looking at his assistant with a puzzled frown.

"First of all, Elaine Parker's pregnancy." Storm's eyes gleamed. "Your tight little group didn't think we knew about that, but Paul Kendell knew and told us."

Paul glanced around the room, almost smirking. "They didn't know that I knew either," he said, "but you can't photograph a woman for weeks on end and not notice a thing like that." His pale eyes settled on Neil. "I thought that was why you killed her."

Bob sat in his chair, staring down at the old straw rug, as though he didn't care what was going on around him, and the inspector, following his lead, spoke as though he were not present.

"We know, of course," he said, "that Elaine claimed Neil Stratton tried to kill her about a week before she disappeared, and it seemed strange that everyone we questioned was sure she seemed to really believe it, while he seemed equally honest in denying it. But there were two factors that never seemed to have occurred to any of you."

Andrew's chin went up as though his integrity had been challenged. "What factors, Inspector?"

"That someone else could have tried to drown Elaine that night and that the baby was not necessarily Neil Stratton's."

A hush came over the room. Nancy, glancing sideways, saw Neil turn dead white and felt his body close to hers stiffen. He was staring at his old friend.

"Was it yours, Bob?" he asked, his voice husky.

Bob raised his head and looked back at Neil, his expression sad but also angry. "Yes, but it's not the way you think it was, Neil."

"Then why don't you tell him how it really was," Inspector Storm said.

Bob kept his eyes on Neil. "It all began when I met Elaine in the office. I didn't know then that she was a nympho and I fell for her like a ton of bricks, just as you did later, and again, like you, when she told me she was pregnant, I asked her to marry me."

"Then why didn't she?" Neil asked, looking skeptical.

"Because she suddenly cooled off and told me it was all over. She said she was going to get rid of the baby and didn't want to see me any more. I couldn't understand what had happened, but just then the firm sent me to Dallas on a long-drawn-out tax case. When I got back in July, I found out that you were seeing her."

Bob raised his handcuffed wrists, trying to adjust his glasses, then turned to the inspector. "Can you take these damned things off? They're driving me crazy."

The handcuffs were removed and Bob went on. "I was still terribly in love with her, so I came out here one night when I knew you were going to the hospital to see Nellie and I begged her to come back to me." Bob's face hardened. "She told me she was going to marry you. It damned near killed me."

"Oh, my God," Neil said, and looked away.

Bob continued, driving himself relentlessly, as though he

had to prove that the blame for everything lay with Elaine, not him.

"I had a vacation coming up, so I went up to my family's place in Maine, but I couldn't get over Elaine, so on my way back, I thought I'd stop by and try once more. It was around the middle of August then and I didn't dream she was still pregnant. Believe me."

Neil nodded. "I do, Bob. Go on."

"I knew you were spending your weekends with her, but I thought you would have gone back to the city by late Sunday night, so I planned to stop by after you had left. There were lights on in the house, so I parked up on the road and went to the front door. Nobody answered and the door was locked, but I knew Elaine liked to sit out on the sun deck on moonlight nights, so I went around the house."

Bob was gripping the arms of his chair by then and so pale he looked ill. Oliver pulled his flask from his pocket and splashed some into the jelly glass he still held in his hand, then looked at Inspector Storm, who nodded. The drink down, some of the color returned to Bob's face and he drove himself on, talking exclusively to Neil, as though they were alone in the room, his manner a queer mixture of hostility and regret.

"I didn't know you were still there until I heard voices; then while I was trying to decide what to do, I realized that you were having a violent argument. I heard Elaine scream that it was too late for her to have an abortion, that she didn't believe in them and would never have one." Bob's voice rose angrily. "I knew then that she was passing the baby off on you to get you to marry her. All because of your goddamned money."

Neil frowned. "But she never knew about that. For God's sake, I didn't even know myself."

"She knew, but I didn't know how she had found out until I remembered that she had been in the office one day while I was still going around with her. She often dropped by and we would go out to lunch and that day I was working on Nellie's accounts. I was called out of the office for some reason and put the accounts in a desk drawer before I left. When I came back she was over by the desk, pretending to look out the window. It never dawned on me that she'd looked into the file until I heard her insisting that you marry her. Then I saw the whole picture. She knew that your grandmother had a fortune and you were going to inherit it."

"Then what happened?" Inspector Storm asked.

A look of utter hatred came over Bob's face. "I stood there, frozen. I couldn't believe it; then I remembered Neil telling me that he had run into Elaine by accident outside of his office. Like hell he did. She arranged it." His eyes went back to Neil. "Just like she arranged to dump me and go after you for your money."

"Let's get back to that night you overheard the argument and knew the truth," the inspector said impatiently.

"Well, I was still standing there when I saw Elaine run down to the beach and start walking. I wanted to follow her, but I was afraid Neil would go after her, so I waited until I saw a light go on in an upstairs bedroom."

"Why in God's name didn't you come up and tell me?" Neil asked.

"I guess I was too furious to make sense. All I could think of was having it out with Elaine. I waited until your light went off, then I saw her coming back, but she didn't come to the house. She went out to the dock. I followed her and by the time I came up behind her, I was in a blinding rage."

The inspector stopped in the midst of lighting a cigarette. "Did you say anything to her?"

Bob nodded. "I meant to confront her with it, but suddenly all I wanted to do was kill her. I couldn't help it. I grabbed her and screamed that she was never going to marry

Neil, then threw her into the water and held her down. Later, I found out that she thought it was Neil saying he was never going to marry her."

Neil's eyes were glazed as he looked at Bob. "Did you think you had killed her when you let go?"

"No, I couldn't go through with it. I let her go, then ran back to my car and drove into the city."

Andrew Crawford got up and went over to Bob, his face anxious and puzzled. "I can understand how you must have felt, but why on earth didn't you leave it at that? Why kill her?"

For the first time, Bob looked ashamed. "I didn't want to and I felt rotten when I heard she was going all over town accusing Neil of trying to kill her, but I knew he'd have money enough to take care of himself, while my career would be ruined if I'd told anybody the truth."

"It would have been better to take that risk."

"You don't understand, sir," Bob said, running his fingers through his hair. "I heard that she had closed the house and moved into the Drake and that she was planning to leave town to get away from Neil."

Andrew shrugged. "So what? Good riddance."

"For God's sake, she was still carrying my child and that was worrying the hell out of me. I was still trying to figure out what to do about it on that morning of August twenty-second, when she suddenly turned up bag and baggage. She said she was leaving town and needed money, but I didn't have enough. Then she said she thought she knew where she could raise it and asked me if she could leave her luggage at the apartment. She said she'd be back for it at about six; then she left and I went to the office as usual."

"Isn't it strange that she should turn to you?" Andrew asked.

Bob shook his head. "She didn't have the faintest idea that I knew she was still carrying my child. I sweated blood all day, then decided to tell her I knew, and ask her what she planned to do about it. When she got back, I made a couple of drinks and sprang it on her. I asked her flatly what she was going to do."

Bob's cold eyes stared up at his boss. "She told me that I couldn't prove it was mine and that she intended to have the baby, then sue Neil for paternity and get everything she could out of him."

There was a stunned silence in the room. Andrew, looking old and tired, returned to the sofa and sat down beside Kate.

"That did it," Bob said, as though determined to get the thing over with. "I went crazy and before I knew it, I had her by the throat." He glanced up at the inspector standing by the hearth. "You were right about the rest."

"I know." Storm looked grim. "You took your car out of the garage on East Sixty-ninth Street at ten that night and did not return until seven the next morning. I presume you waited until very late, then loaded the woman and her luggage and drove out here. Your apartment is on the ground floor and if someone had noticed you, you would have pretended she was drunk."

Bob's face was very pale again and still angry. "The damned bitch didn't deserve to live. She was a monster."

Inspector Storm's eyes turned icy. "Maybe she was, but Vicky Colton wasn't and neither was that poor, destitute reporter." He paused, then said, "Miss Colton knew that it was you and not Neil Stratton who was responsible for Elaine's pregnancy, didn't she?"

"Yes," Bob said wearily, "but I didn't know it until Kate threw that party for Oliver's sister. I was standing by my boss and Vicky and I heard him tell her about it. I saw the shocked look on her face, then heard her say she thought they should stall Elaine's father until they could check further."

"He wanted to start an investigation into his daughter's disappearance," Andrew explained.

The inspector nodded, then looked at Bob. "Go on, Ewing."

"Well, I moved off, but I saw Vicky staring at me, and I suddenly realized that she knew the truth; then I remembered the day Elaine dumped me. We'd had a luncheon date and she came by to pick me up as usual, but it turned out that she had come to tell me she was through and was going to have an abortion. We had a scene and Vicky must have overheard it. Her office is . . . was between Andrew Crawford's and mine."

"But she never discussed it with you?" Inspector Storm asked.

"No, she must have assumed as I did that Elaine had gotten rid of the baby before she started her affair with Neil."

"Then what?"

"Then I saw Vicky leave the room and I followed her to that little office of Kate's off the hall and I heard her talking to Neil and I knew she was going to tell him." Bob pushed up his glasses and rubbed his eyes. "I was afraid that if she did, they would start investigating me and the whole thing would come out."

Storm's eyes flashed. "So you beat your friend down to Miss Colton's apartment and killed her."

Bob swallowed hard and nodded.

"But why the reporter?" Andrew asked, looking outraged.

"I don't know why he was tailing Neil," Bob said, "but that night when you and I left Neil's apartment I went down with you to help fight off the reporters. Remember?"

"Of course," Andrew snapped.

"Well, after you got into a cab, one of the reporters came up to me and got me aside. He recognized me as Neil's attorney, because of all the publicity the year before, when

I was with him during a lot of press and television interviews. Walsh told me that he had followed Neil down to Vicky's apartment and could testify that he was in the clear, but wouldn't open his mouth unless he received ten thousand dollars by midnight."

"But you didn't want Neil Stratton cleared," Storm said harshly. "You wanted to keep him on ice in case you came under suspicion yourself. So you told Walsh you would meet him in the Park and then knifed him."

Bob seemed to be getting nervous and tired. "Yes, but who in hell put the guy on Neil in the first place?"

The inspector's eyes went to Paul Kendell, whose face had suddenly become almost as pale as Bob's.

"Care to answer that, Mr. Kendell? You are the only person in this case who had any association with Irving Walsh. You and he were in the same graduating class at CCNY."

Paul seemed surprised for a minute; then a touch of his arrogance returned. "All right, I did get Walsh to tail Neil and start asking questions. It was his idea to use a fake name, but with Nancy probing into her cousin's disappearance, I thought things were finally coming to a head. I was sure Neil had done something terrible to Elaine and would get away with it, so I thought that if Walsh hounded him and kept asking questions, he would know someone was suspicious of him. I thought we might wear him down and he would crack under the pressure."

Nancy, who had been sitting quietly beside Neil, leaned forward and glared at Paul. "And you tried to make me think he was guilty too, didn't you?"

Paul looked at her and then at Neil. "I'm sorry, really, but I thought I was doing Walsh a favor, that if he stuck it out, he'd get a story when it broke and, if it didn't, I would pay him for his time."

"Some favor you did him," Inspector Storm remarked dryly.

The photographer's thin face flushed and he looked down at his hands.

There was a tense silence in the room; then Bob Ewing suddenly jumped out of his chair and started for the door to the sun deck. The detective who had been standing by the chair was after him instantly, his gun drawn. So was the man who had been sitting beside Paul Kendell. There was a brief struggle; then Bob was again in handcuffs, held between the two detectives, his eyes wild.

"I can't stand any more of this," he screamed. "I've got to get out of here."

"Very well," Inspector Storm said calmly, then glanced at his men. "Take him to Headquarters. I'll be along soon."

Nancy watched them until the front door closed behind them; then she turned to Storm. "I know you used me as some kind of bait tonight, Inspector, but I don't understand why," she said.

The inspector seemed to relax. "We suspected Ewing for several reasons. We knew he had taken his car out on the night your cousin disappeared and that he had been on more than casual terms with her. His neighbors had seen her leave his apartment several mornings early that spring. We knew quite a bit, but we couldn't prove anything, so we laid a trap."

"I still don't understand," Nancy said.

"The dog. If it hadn't been for him, we might never have nailed Ewing." The inspector came close to smiling. "Ewing probably thought he had killed him, or that somebody would just take him away, and he must have been horrified when he found out that Neil Stratton had taken the dog home with him."

Nancy continued to look bewildered. "You mean André . . . ?"

"I mean André is no dumb, cringing little poodle, but a big brave dog with enough guts to try to defend his mistress from a killer. He would never forget who that was and if he ever saw the man again, he would attack again, which meant that Ewing, who had been a close friend of Neil Stratton's for several years and a frequent visitor, could never go near the penthouse again as long as the dog was there."

Andrew looked disgusted. "It's a wonder he didn't try to kill the poor pup."

Storm nodded. "He might have tried it, but it's not so easy to get into a well-guarded building these days without being announced, so he found an easier way. He lied."

"About what?" Nancy asked.

Inspector Storm looked at Miss Hilton, who was still sitting on the sofa beside Kate, cool and detached.

"Madge Hilton is a policewoman who works for our department. We've had Ewing's phone tapped at home and Madge has been recording his office calls and private conversations as well."

Oliver looked amused. "So, that's why she wouldn't take a drink," he said. "She was on duty."

The inspector smiled faintly, then went on, "We know that when Mrs. Colton's friend Mrs. Peterson came to settle Vicky's affairs and take her body back to Ohio, she didn't know what was to be done about the dog until she got back home and talked to Mrs. Colton. Ewing couldn't lie about that, because a friend of Vicky's from the office was there and heard the conversation. So he waited."

"He told me that if Mrs. Peterson didn't call him, he would call her this morning," Nancy said.

"He did make the call," Storm said, "but not from the office, where Madge could monitor it. The first she heard of it was when she heard him tell Andrew Crawford that he had phoned Mrs. Peterson and she had told him Mrs. Colton was going to retire and wanted the dog because he had belonged to her daughter."

"And I believed it implicitly," Andrew said wryly.

Inspector Storm lit another cigarette and frowned. "Madge reported to me immediately and I asked her to check with Mrs. Peterson, but she hit a snag."

Miss Hilton nodded. "The hospital wouldn't let me talk to Mrs. Colton and I couldn't locate Mrs. Peterson." She smiled at Nancy. "When Mr. Crawford was advising you not to try and buy the dog, I was dying to tell you to wait until we could verify Ewing's story, but I couldn't, of course."

Storm took it from there. "When Madge finally reached Mrs. Peterson she said that Ewing had called and she had told him that Mrs. Colton was going back to work as soon as she was well enough and did *not* want the dog."

Nancy was suddenly furious. All the rest of it seemed like some horrible nightmare, but André was very real to her.

"Do you mean he was going to have someone crate André and take him away, pretending he was going to Ohio, then get rid of him?"

"Yes," the inspector said. "Then you loused up his plans. No one else questioned him, but you wanted to buy the dog and Andrew Crawford, not knowing then what was going on, tried to keep you from interfering."

"He almost succeeded," Nancy said, giving Andrew a reproachful look.

Andrew smiled grimly. "I didn't know then that Bob had lied, my dear. I didn't know until Inspector Storm came to the office later and outlined his plan to force a confession out of him. Then we arranged with Kate to have that little party tonight, so that I could get you back on the subject of the dog in Bob's presence."

"Then all that talk about getting a puppy was part of it?"

"Yes," Andrew said, waving his cigar. "And you played it up beautifully, as we hoped you would, insisting that you were still going to try and get André, while Ewing couldn't help hearing it. We figured that if he was sure you were going to call Ohio and find out he had lied, he would go to any extreme to stop you."

The inspector took over again. "You see, Miss Gilbert, the dog was the only witness to any of Ewing's crimes and if you had found out that Mrs. Colton did not want her daughter's dog, you would have known instantly why he had lied. Only one person would have any reason to want the dog done away with . . . Vicky Colton's murderer."

Nancy frowned, still puzzled. "But how did Bob know I would be coming out here?"

Kate Vail leaned forward. "That was my part. Bob knew there was something more up than Neil's being late for dinner, so he was hanging around outside the dining room while I was talking to you. I was facing the hall, if you remember, and I made sure he would hear me when I asked you about Neil and then offered you my car." She looked unhappy. "If he hadn't been there, I was to tell him. I even arranged for a delay in getting the car brought around in order to give Bob time to get here, following the inspector's instructions."

"Nobody wanted to do it this way, Miss Gilbert," Storm said, "but it was our only hope of trapping Ewing and getting a confession out of him."

"I understand," Nancy said, then turned to Neil. "And that phone call to Mrs. Mallory was faked too?"

Neil put his arm around her. "We knew she would get in touch with you if she was really worried about me. My phone is bugged and if she hadn't reached you, I would have called you at Kate's, but it sounded more realistic coming from her."

"Will someone kindly explain something to me?" Oliver Vail suddenly asked.

Inspector Storm nodded. "Shoot."

"If Bob expected Neil to be here, how did he think he could get away with attacking Nancy?"

"He probably planned to take care of Neil before Nancy got here, perhaps just knock him out, so that he could pin her death on him too," Storm said. "The men who tailed him said he drove like a madman, and we had opened a window there by the front door. He used it and cased the house before he went outside."

"My God," Andrew said. "It's almost impossible to believe that a fellow like Bob . . ."

Inspector Storm nodded. "He undoubtedly killed Elaine Parker in a fit of rage, but from then on he was out to save his own hide at anybody's expense." He glanced around the room, looking tired but pleased. "I guess that wraps it up, and I want to thank you all for your help."

Neil drove Nancy back to the city. They sat very close together and did not talk much, both still shocked and depressed by all that had been revealed that evening; then as they crossed Central Park on their way to Fifth Avenue, Nancy perked up.

"Let's go to your place and have a drink," she said. "I don't feel like being alone."

He couldn't have agreed more and a few minutes later they were in the living room of the penthouse having drinks in front of the fire Neil had just lit. Nancy was staring at the flames and frowning.

"Didn't it ever occur to you that Elaine's baby might not have been yours?" she asked.

Neil flushed and shook his head. "I realize now that the timing was off. I should have known from her figure and other things that she was too far along for it to have been mine, but I never questioned it at all. I wasn't as smart as poor Vicky."

"What are your plans now?"

"To make a settlement on that reporter's widow, first of

all, then make sure that Vicky's mother has everything she needs."

Nancy smiled. "That's what I'd hoped you would say."

He smiled back and hugged her. "Then we'll get married and build a house in the country and I'll plant a million flowers for you and a lovely lawn for André to play on."

"And a big kitchen for Mrs. Mallory if she's still speaking to you after that phone call you faked."

Neil got up and laughed. "Come on, let's go wake them up and tell them."

Neither of them mentioned Elaine and they never would again, and Nancy had already decided to give the Parker property to the town of Westport so that the public could enjoy the beach, as though it might somehow make up for the tragedy her cousin's greed had caused.

She got up and kissed Neil. "Let's go!"

NO RENEWALS!

PLEASE RETURN BOOK AND REQUEST AGAIN.